KRAKEN VS. MEGALODON

Eric S Brown

SEVERED PRESS
HOBART TASMANIA

KRAKEN VS. MEGALODON

KRAKEN VS. MEGALODON

The water was dark, but Kaliner knew that it wasn't cold. Not that he could feel it. He relied on the data from his suit's sensors to gauge its temp. His suit was environmentally sealed. It wasn't quite power armor like one would see in a science fiction film, but it was close. An APS-2 rifle was affixed to the side of the air tank on the suit's back, and a PPS-4 pistol was holstered on the armor plating that covered his hip. He could see Greg in the distance, standing beside a crevice in the ocean floor. The two of them had been dispatched to make sure the quake Atlantis Alpha had picked up hadn't done anything in the region that would cause problems. The two of them had spent most of yesterday checking Atlantis Alpha's exterior for damage. It had checked out clear. The science geeks were reporting that there was a temperature in this area, though, and it needed to be checked out as well.

"Thermal readings are higher over here," Greg's voice crackled over the comm in Kaliner's suit.

Greg's heavy footsteps stirred silt as he marched towards Greg. "You're not saying we need to go in there are you?" he asked.

"Nah," Greg answered. "Check your sensors, man. The only thing that could be causing the spike in temps here is magma down there somewhere, let loose by the quake. It'll cool eventually."

Kaliner could see Greg shaking his head as he reached Greg's position at the edge of the crevice.

"Sometimes you have to wonder why they even send us to check on things like this," Greg sighed.

"Just two more weeks," Kaliner said.

He heard Greg laugh over the comm. "Hard to believe it's been nearly six months already."

"Oh, I believe it." Kaliner popped the magnetic lock keeping the control module for the mini-pod held to the upper right side of his suit. "I can feel it in my bones. Gonna have nightmares about this place when I get back on land."

Both he and Greg were Navy. Neither of them had much choice about being part of Atlantis Alpha's team. Kaliner remembered how excited he had been at first when he received his orders. It hadn't taken long for that magic to wear off as he realized he was going to be nothing more than grunt labor for the geeks that ran the project. And grunt labor they had been. They had worked harder than Kaliner would have imagined possible. Anytime the geeks needed something fetched from the ocean, something needed to be fixed on Atlantis Alpha's exterior, or they needed something checked out, it was him and Greg who were sent out in the mini-pod to get the job done. It was like a never-ending "honey-do" list and a crappy one, too. That wasn't to say the gig was all bad, though.

Kaliner paused to look around him before keying in the code to bring the mini-pod to active status and set it on a course to pick them up. The ocean was beautiful even way down here. That was when it struck Kaliner that they were alone. The normal bottom life of the region was nowhere to be seen. Maybe the quake had frightened them into hiding, but he doubted it. Still, he would have expected the fish to have returned to their normal patterns by now.

The headlights of the mini-pod slashed through the darkness as it came racing through the water and then slowed to settle on the ocean floor for the two of them to enter it.

"Something wrong?" Greg asked.

"Nothing moving down here today," Kaliner answered. "It's just creeping me out a little is all."

"Fine by me," Greg snorted. "The fish down here are as ugly as they come. I am totally cool with not having to see them."

Kaliner chuckled. "Beauty is in the eye of the beholder, buddy."

"Whatever," Greg grunted. "Let's get out of here."

Both Kaliner and Greg headed for the mini-pod.

Greg paused. "Kaliner, you picking up something weird over that ridge there?"

Kaliner checked his sensor data. "I am reading movement." Kaliner rechecked the data. "Whatever it is…"

"It's huge," Greg finished for him.

"One of ours?" Kaliner asked.

"Can't be," Greg answered.

Kaliner was already detaching his APS rifle and readying it as Greg started for the mini-pod. "What are you doing?"

Greg paused. "I don't know about you, but I ain't getting paid enough to see what's on the other side of the ridge in person. We check it out, we're using the pod. As large as whatever is over there is, that rifle of yours isn't going to do anything more than tick it off."

Kaliner glanced down at the rifle he held. Greg just might be right this time. He reattached the rifle to his suit and lumbered on after Greg. The two of them entered the pod's airlock. As soon as the water was flushed from it, Kaliner popped his helmet. He took a breath of the pod's air.

The mini-pod was roughly three times the size of a van. There was the airlock, the van-sized interior of the pilot and work compartment, and the rest of its space belonged to its engines. Kaliner and Greg hurried to strap into their seats at the pod's controls. Kaliner killed the automatic pilot remote functions that the pod had been operating under and switched its systems over to manual.

"We got eighty-two percent power," Kaliner said with a grin as he engaged the pod's engines and it rose from the ocean floor.

"Bringing primary sensor array online," Greg told him.

"Run an active sweep of the ridge," Kaliner ordered.

"Already on it." Greg replied, nodding as Kaliner glanced over at him.

Kaliner maneuvered the pod in the water, so its front faced the distant ridge line. It floated in the water like a hovering helicopter would in the sky. Kaliner had shut down the pod's forward lights as he didn't want it to be an easy target should whatever was on the other side of the ridge decide to come out fighting.

The pod was equipped with twin, forward-facing torpedo tubes. They were a last ditch defensive precaution as the pod wasn't designed for combat. Each tube only contained a single torpedo with no reloads aboard the craft. Their yield was far less than that of a standard torpedo, but they still packed a punch. They were made to engage large, threatening sea life, not enemy ships. Flipping a switch on the controls in front of him with his thumb, Kaliner armed them.

"Any data on the contact?" Kaliner asked.

"Whatever it is, it's biologic in nature."

Kaliner had already known that. Sure, Atlantis Alpha's research was insanely valuable, and there were those who would go to great lengths to obtain it, but it was also extremely classified. Very few knew Atlantis Alpha existed, much less of the work being done inside the base. Beyond that, Atlantis Alpha had technology that was well ahead of the curve and classified as well. For a rival government or corporation to be able to field operatives this far down, well, it was unlikely. The sensor data on their suits had already confirmed the thing on the other side of the ridge wasn't one of Atlantis Alpha's creations. Its signature was all wrong, and it had no ID transponder. Everything that Atlantis Alpha let loose into the water was tagged and carefully kept track of.

"That's such a big help," Kaliner quipped. "Got anything else?"

Greg didn't answer him. The man was staring straight ahead through the pod's forward observation window. He had gone pale and was trembling in his seat.

Kaliner turned his gaze forward again just in time to see death coming at him. His last thought was of his home in North Carolina before the pod exploded in a flash of light and muffled flames.

****

Ensign Robert Waters sat at the sensor console in Atlantis Alpha's command room. His shift had been a long one, and he was ready for it to be over with. Everything was as boring as usual since the small quake. With Atlantis Alpha's "children" away with DESRON 49, there wasn't much to keep track of this far down in the water. The top of his console was lined with toys. Waters had loved superheroes since he was a little boy growing up in Idaho. He reached out and picked up an action figure of a gray-clad cowboy. The cowboy clutched a six-shooter in his tiny hand. Waters stared at the cowboy's scarred face and smiled, remembering a storyline in which the character had killed one of the most powerful heroes in comics with a radioactive bullet. The cowboy always reminded Waters never to underestimate the underdog.

Waters had grown up on a farm in the middle of nowhere and came from a long line of farmers. Neither his mom nor his dad had wanted him to leave and attend college. He wasn't like his brother and two sisters who were content with life in the country. Waters wanted more out of life. Much to the disappointment of his parents, he spent most of his childhood reading rather than in the fields. Oh, he had pulled his weight on the farm, his father hadn't given him any choice in that, but his free time belonged to folks like Verne, Wells, and Lovecraft.

As soon as he was of age, Waters had left the farm behind and joined the Navy. It was the best thing that ever happened to him. The Navy paid for his college and he got to see the world, and more importantly, the oceans. *Twenty Thousand Leagues Under the Sea* was his all-time favorite novel. He identified with the adventurous spirit of Captain Nemo and the crew of the Nautilus.

His talent for machines and computers served him well in both college and his stint in the Navy. Now, he worked freelance as one of the best sonar techs in the world. The Atlantis Corporation had snatched him up for this project, and he was glad to be here despite the monotony of his work at times. The amount he got paid in a month was as much as his father made in a year. The thought of that made the smile on his lips grow even wider. Just like the character the action figure he held in his hands represented, he had overcome the odds and made something of himself that he could be happy with and proud of.

"Waters!" he heard Commander Burke shout from behind him. "What in the devil are you doing?"

Waters swiveled around his chair to face the commander. "Sir?"

The command room of Atlantis Alpha wasn't huge. It contained only four workstations and the station's command chair where Burke sat. The weapons and engineering stations were currently vacant. Only Sam, at the communications console, shared the room with the two of them. Atlantis Alpha was a fixed base, so there was no reason to have someone at the other stations except during times of need or crisis.

He glanced quickly at Sam. She had her hair pulled up today atop her head. It was a deep red that heavily contrasted the paleness of her skin. She was several years younger than he was but that only added how enticing she was. An air of innocence clung to her like a thick perfume, though Waters knew from experience that she was no such thing.

"Waters, I asked you a question," Burke's voice echoed off the walls of the command room, rising in volume.

Waters realized he was still holding the action figure and tried to hide it as much as he could with his hands before he answered, "Uh, nothing, sir."

He felt Burke's gaze burning into him as the commander asked, "What's the status of the pod Kaliner and Greg took out this morning? Are they inbound yet?"

Waters stuck the pointer finger of his right hand up and into the air. "One moment, sir," he said and spun his chair back around. He checked his screens before he answered, "No sign of them, sir."

Kaliner and Greg often went "off the reservation" though, so Waters wasn't too concerned. Though Atlantis Alpha's sensors were top of the line, there were still a lot of things on the ocean floor that could prevent them from giving a good reading at longer distances. If the guys had landed the pod and had it in lower-power mode or ventured into one of the ravines that were everywhere down here, there was a good chance he wasn't going to get a clear reading on them.

"They missed their last check in," Sam reminded Burke.

Waters shot her a scowl and wondered if she was just trying to make his life miserable. Dealing with Burke was one of the few bad things about this job, and on the worse days, Waters really wanted to wipe the smug look from Burke's face with his knuckles.

"I'm sure they're…" Waters started, but Burke interrupted him.

"Stop playing with those toys and do your job, Waters," Burke growled. "Find me that pod. Now."

Waters swallowed hard, forcing himself to hold his temper in check. He brought Atlantis Alpha's sensors up to active level and started sweeping the water for any sign of the pod.

"Unknown contact!" Waters shouted, his eyes bugging at what he saw on his screens. "CBDR at twenty knots. ETA in five!"

Burke threw himself forward in his chair. "What do you mean unknown?"

"Just what I said, sir!" Waters snapped. "Unknown. It's registering as biologic in nature but…"

"But what?" Sam asked before Burke could.

"Whatever it is, it's bigger than the largest battle carrier the US has at her disposal." Waters kept his eyes glued to his screens watching the contact close on Atlantis Alpha.

"That's impossible!" Burke blurted. "Get me Smith up here ASAP! Hyde too! He's going to want to see whatever is out there!"

Smith was Atlantis Alpha's weapons officer and security chief. A buff, crude, ex-Marine dude who had a lot in common with Burke despite the tattoos that covered his body. Hyde was Burke's nickname for Doctor John Hydely, who was the chief scientist aboard the base. It was his ideas that the whole operation was created around. Hydely was a wizard at genetic engineering and marine biology. If anyone knew what the contact approaching Atlantis Alpha was, it would be him.

As Sam began paging for Dr. Hydely, Smith bolted into the command room. She had paged him first. He took his seat at the weapons station, bringing it online.

"What's going on?" Smith asked.

"Inbound contact," Waters told him. "Not one of ours. Given its size and speed, I don't think the commander wants us taking any chances."

"I'm right behind you, Waters," Burke roared. "Smith, take that thing out there with guns and convince it that it doesn't want to come anywhere near us."

"Yes, sir," Smith replied, nodding.

Atlantis Alpha was equipped with multiple torpedo tubes as well as underwater cannons that could spew a good deal of hot rounds into the waters surrounding the base. The cannons lacked the amount of sheer firepower that a surface ship's C.I.W.S. possessed, but they could cut the side of a sperm whale to pieces with a single burst. They were designed for close-in defense, so just as Waters figured, Smith opened with a volley of torpedoes.

Waters watched the torpedoes streak through the ocean towards their target. Smith couldn't have missed if he had wanted to, considering the size of the approaching contact. Both torpedoes scored direct hits on the unknown contact. The sound of their detonations rang in the headphones that now covered Waters' ears.

"Both torpedoes are direct hits!" Waters reported. "Contact appears undamaged. They don't appear to have even slowed it, sir."

At that exact moment, Dr. Hydely entered the command room. His eyes darted about as he appeared to take in the panic of those around him. Waters could see the doctor wanted to ask what was happening, but Hydely wisely kept his mouth shut. He moved to stand beside Burke's command chair.

Waters knew Atlantis Alpha was one of the toughest built structures in the world, but he didn't know if it would hold up should that thing out there ram it. Counting those currently in the room with him, there were nearly two dozen personnel aboard the station. It was up to Burke and Smith to keep them all alive. Somehow, that didn't fill Waters with overwhelming confidence.

The unknown contact was less than a minute and a half away now and increasing speed. Waters realized it had to be in range of the base's exterior cameras and called up a visual from them on his screen. His heart skipped a beat in his chest as he saw the contact, or rather, part of it. Smith had let loose on the monster with the base's cannons and high velocity; underwater rounds ripped and tore at the thing's flesh, filling the water outside the Atlantis Alpha with a thick, oil-like blood. The black blood swirled about in the water as rounds continued to tear into the approaching monster. There really was no other word to describe the thing better than monster that Waters could think of as he stared at its gigantic form.

The base's cannons were having no more effect on the monster than the volley of torpedoes had. There seemed to be no stopping it.

"Brace for impact!" Burke yelled.

Then the monster struck Atlantis Alpha, and Waters' world went dark.

****

Commodore Blanton stood on the command deck of the USS *Rom*. She was the first of her kind. The USS *Rom* was the prototype of a new class of cruiser that put all her predecessors to shame. She was as fast and agile as the destroyers of DESRON 13 that surrounded her and yet dwarfed them in terms of firepower. Regardless of how impressive she was on paper, though, Commodore Blanton still had his doubts about her. There had been no time for a proper shakedown cruise. Her crew, shoved together in haste, also left him wondering about the wisdom of the powers that be assigning her as DESRON 13's flagship for this mission. He'd read over his orders and the reports that had been handed to him before DESRON 13 made for open water and understood the likely need for the additional firepower she could bring to bear, but that didn't mean he was happy about it.

Only the officers of DESRON 13 knew the nature of the mission ahead of them, and even that info was on a need-to-know basis according to rank. Apparently, the Navy and an unspecified corporation had gone in together to create a new type of weapon. Blanton had heard whispers of the project behind closed doors, but he never fully believed there was any merit to the rumors until he received his current orders. Project Megalodons was very real. A scientist named Hydely had discovered a means in which to create megalodons and train them to act as coherent strike forces under guided direction. The uses of such tech were staggering and could possibly give the United States complete control of the oceans if it were to be fully implanted. Hydely's megalodons were much more than just giant sharks. There was no indication of the exact number of megalodons Hydely had already created, but Blanton got the feeling that it was far more than just a few.

Doctor Hydely's research was conducted beneath the waves for the most part at a corporate-owned facility called Atlantis Alpha. All contact with the underwater base had been lost two days ago. DESRON 49, which wasn't technically a full DESRON, had been assigned to assist Dr. Hydely and was away from the location of the Atlantis Alpha base when contact with it had been lost. The DESRON 49 was under strict orders to keep its existence secret, and as thus, all attempts to make contact with it had failed as well. The powers that be suspected that DESRON 49 would return to the location of the Atlantis Alpha base given time, assuming it was still out there and hadn't been destroyed.

The most likely explanation of the loss of communications with Atlantis Alpha was that Dr. Hydely's pet megalodons had gone rouge, overriding their commands somehow, and turning on their keepers. DESRON 13 had been dispatched to assess the situation and do what needed to be done if Hydely's pets had become free-willed monsters. There could be no trace of the experiments conducted at the Atlantis Alpha base left to fall into hands other than those belonging to the United States Navy. Commodore Blanton dreaded facing the megalodons if they had indeed gone rogue. There was no information regarding the creatures' exact capabilities or if the good doctor had outfitted them with any rather nasty surprises beyond making them stronger, larger, and faster. The powers that be, though, had faith that the USS *Rom*, combined with the other ships that composed DESRON 13, would be more than enough to deal with them. Blanton at least knew what he was facing, and that alone gave him an edge.

DESRON 13 was proceeding to the coordinates where Atlantis Alpha was located beneath the waves at near full speed. Blanton didn't want to push the ships of the DESRON any harder than he had to, but his orders also required him to wrap the whole mess up as quickly as possible. The last thing he wanted was to arrive with his ships on the edge of experiencing mechanical issues, and the *Rom* was already approaching that. Her fancy new engine was still getting its bugs worked out.

Commodore Blanton supposed he could have gone in search of DESRON 49 first, but that would have taken time. The location of Atlantis Alpha was exact, and for all the danger that a group of loose, genetically engineered, and weaponized megalodons posed, the data contained in the base's computers and Doctor Hydely's notes was a far greater threat.

"Sir?" his XO, Allen, said as she walked up to stand next to him.

Blanton hadn't really gotten used to calling her Allen yet. Henrietta Allen was the sort of XO every captain dreamed of, if that dream included a stripper's pole and lurid sex scenes. She was only twenty-four years old, and her body was both hard and soft in all the right places. The standard-issue command uniform she wore did nothing but perhaps enhance her appearance. Her blonde hair was short and "bob cut" above her shoulders. It fell, hanging tight, to the curse of her face. Sharp blue eyes full of strength and intelligence met his gaze, and he knew he had been caught checking her out. He wasn't a lecherous man by nature. His feelings towards Allen were something he was going need to address before he ended up being court-martialed for inappropriate behavior.

Clearing his throat, Blanton did his utmost best not to blush. He was old enough to be her father, not to mention he was her commanding officer.

"Yes, Allen?" he said at last. "What can I do for you?"

"We'll be arriving above Atlantis Alpha in ten minutes," Allen informed him. "Deep sonar scans reveal that the base is still intact, though heavily damaged. We continue to be unable to raise the base on any channel. If there is anyone left alive down there, sir, they aren't answering our hails."

"Get Nicolson and his team ready," Blanton ordered. "I want them to be ready to hit the water the moment we reach the base."

Allen turned and left to carry his order as Blanton forced himself not to watch her hips as she walked away. He kept his eyes forward, looking out the forward window of the *Rom*'s bridge. When Allen was out of earshot, he let out a sigh of relief and relaxed a bit. Just like being ordered to deal with a group of weaponized megalodons, dealing with an XO like Allen was an utterly new and certainly challenging experience. He was thankful she hadn't called him on his behavior, and hoped that meant she was giving him time to sort out whatever was going on inside him rather than taking notes to press charges against him when DESRON 13's mission was completed.

****

Lieutenant Darin Nicholson was at the helm of Pod I when it splashed into the water. It was the command pod of the three submersibles deployed by DESRON 13 to investigate what had transpired at the Atlantis Alpha base. All three pods were cutting edge and used the same tech that the deep sea pods of the base itself did.

Jeff Lyle sat beside Nicholson in the pod's copilot seat. Nicholson could see that Lyle was having a tough time of it. Lyle was much more of a hands-on sort of guy; needing to use the pod was getting to him.

"We'll be there before you know it," Nicholson told him and kicked the pod's engines to full as he opened a combat channel to the other pods. "Engines at full. Maximum descent," he ordered the others.

"Yes, sir," Graham replied from Pod II.

"You got it, boss," Inman answered from Pod III.

The forward lights of the three pods slashed through the underwater darkness as they streaked downward with surprising speed. Atlantis Alpha came into view as the three pods neared the ocean floor. It was a massive, dome-shaped structure. Nicholson adjusted the course of his pod to come in close to it and pass directly in front of the dome. The other pods followed suit, trailing along in its wake. Side beams of light from all three pods played over the base's exterior.

"Holy..." Nicholson heard Lyle mutter. "What in the devil happened down here?"

Nicholson didn't answer. His attention was locked onto the broken and shattered areas of the dome. It looked as if something had used Atlantis Alpha as its own personal punching bag. Entire sections of the base were caved inward. Jagged pieces of shattered metal protruded outward into the water. All of the base's exterior lights were out. There were no signs at all that the base had power, and it was easy to see why. The damage was so extensive it made Nicholson cringe. Lyle's question echoed in his mind as he thought it over for himself. Nicholson had been briefed on Doctor Hydely's experiments and the megalodon threat that could be present in the area. He knew Hydely's creatures had skeletal structures like no normal shark ever would.

They were designed or bred or whatever to ram enemy vessels and survive such strikes. Even so, the damage to Atlantis Alpha didn't have the look of being rammed repeatedly, but rather bashed. The damaged areas were stretched onwards over its surface from the initial point of impact, as if whatever had struck it had continued onward, applying pressure, as it continued to fall onto the base. There were other spots where it looked as if something long and spear-like had punctured the base completely through and then been ripped back out the way it had gone in.

Nicholson didn't care how tough the good doctor's megalodons were or how many of the creatures there were, no shark or sharks, not even super-sized ones, could inflict the type of damage he was seeing.

"Picking up anything?" Nicholson asked Lyle.

"Man, I am picking up all kinds of crazy." Lyle's laughter was sarcastic and bitter. "Could you be a little more exact?"

Nicholson turned his head to give Lyle a quick scowl.

"Whatever hit this base did a heck of a job of wrecking it. You can see just by looking out the window that there are entire sections caved in, and other sections are just gone like they were ripped away. There are unbelievably a few sections of the base where I am picking up power readings. Only one large enough to possibly support life, though. Still, there could be some people left alive in that mess. Most of Atlantis Alpha's insides are flooded, though. It'll take some work to get to the places where there might be survivors."

"Agreed," Inman's voice came over the comm. The other two pods had been listening in on the open combat channel.

Nicholson reached to scratch at his bread. The armored tips of fingers meet the reinforced glass of his face mask to clang against it. Nicholson gave an annoyed grunt as he lowered his hand. Though his team needed the pods to reach Atlantis Alpha as fast as they could, they were all suited up and ready for combat.

"Any working pod docks?" Nicholson asked Lyle.

Lyle took a moment to glance at the data on the screen in front of him. "None," he answered.

Nicholson sighed. It was never easy, was it?

"Everybody, pick a spot as close to the section of the base that still has power as you can. Mag-lock onto the base's hull. Looks like we will be cutting our own doors to get inside, gentlemen."

Half an hour later, Nicholson and Lyle stepped inside Atlantis Alpha. The corridor around them was dark, lit only by the dim red glow of emergency lights. There was water in the corridor as well. It reached their knees as they splashed through it. Nicholson had ordered the crews of Pods II and III to stay aboard their craft until either he gave the all clear or they were needed.

Both he and Lyle carried APS rifles at the ready. Nicholson wasn't taking any chances. He had been through enough situations similar to this one over the years to learn it was best to be ready for anything.

Nicholson led the way with Lyle following close behind. There was just enough space between to them to give Lyle a clear line of fire if something unexpected got the drop on them. According to the pod's sensor data, the space that was most likely where a survivor would be holed up if there was one was just around the bend of the corridor up ahead.

Holding up a hand for Lyle to stay where he was, Nicholson continued forward toward the bend in the corridor. He approached cautiously, but there was no way to do so quietly with the corridor partially flooded. Water sloshed around his boots as he moved. When he reached it, he eased himself around the bend, peering into the darkness beyond. The emergency lights lining the top of the corridor were out in this section, but he could still see a sealed bulkhead door only a few feet from where he stood.

Nicholson gave Lyle the all clear sign and walked up to the door, examining it. There was a keypad on the wall beside it. He sure as Hades didn't have the code needed to open the door and wasn't about to hoof it back to the pod for the cutting gear. Nicholson raised his rifle and slammed its butt into the door. The sound echoed through the corridor. It was his hope that if there was someone alive on the other side, they would open the door when they heard that help had arrived.

Retreating a couple of steps, Nicolson waited to see what happened. He didn't have to wait long. Almost instantly, he heard the servo motors of the doors kick into gear. The door lifted upwards to reveal a man in a blood-smeared lab coat. He looked to be in his early thirties and had the look being an uber nerd about him. The thick-rimmed glasses he wore were taped together between their lenses where they sat on the bridge of his nose. His black, gray-streaked hair was a wet and ruffled mess atop his head.

"Oh thank God!" the man rasped. "I never thought I would see other human beings again."

Nicholson noticed there was a name patch on the lab coat. It read "Hydely."

"Dr. Hydely?" he asked.

"Yes," Hydely answered. "I'm Dr. Hydely. How did you know that?"

"Your name is on your coat." Nicholson smirked. "I'm Lieutenant Nicholson. That guy behind me, you can call him Lyle. We were dispatched as part of DESRON to get you the heck out of here. Are you alone down here?"

"No." Dr. Hydely shook his head. "Ensign Waters survived the attack on Atlantis Alphas as well. Come. He's injured and will need help getting to your pod."

The wide open area Nicholson followed Hydely into was clearly the doctor's personal lab. Ensign Waters lay on an examination table, moaning, appearing to drift in and out of consciousness. Burns covered the flesh of his arms, and his hands were a mangled mess of broken bones and charred tissue.

"The sensor station he was manning when the attack happened blew out," Hydely explained. "I have given him the strongest pain meds I have available but even so…" The doctor left the sentence unfinished.

Lyle moved to lift Ensign Waters from the table as the doctor scurried around the lab, stuffing the pockets of his lab coat full of various crumpled papers and flash drives.

"This is my life's work," he said as Nicholson watched him. "I can't simply leave it all behind."

"Fine by me, Doc," Nicholson said. "Grab what you can, but be quick about it."

As Hydely continued frantically gathering things from around the lab, Nicholson asked, "What happened here, Doc? Did the sharks you were experimenting with turn on you?"

Hydely stopped in his tracks as if someone had punched him in the gut. The look of insult in his expression was profoundly clear.

"No, Lieutenant," he snapped, "they did not. Surely you must know that my megalodons are away from Atlantis Alpha currently. They are engaged in trial maneuvers with DESRON 49."

"Sorry, Doc," Nicholson conceded. "You have to admit, the cliché is that the creations turn on their creator in situations like this one."

Hydely appeared to think over his words, letting them sink in, before he responded, "You are indeed right, Lieutenant

Nicholson, but that is not the case here. My megalodons are as safe as that rifle you are holding in your hands when used correctly."

"Then what did happen here?" Nicholson demanded.

Before Hydely could reply, Lyle butted in. "Uh, boss, this guy here ain't exactly light weight. Can we at least get moving while you grill the doc?"

With a grunt of annoyance, Nicholson nodded. "Anything *inside* this base we should be concerned about on our way out, Doc?"

Doctor Hydely shook his head. "Not that I am aware of, Lieutenant."

"Good," Nicholson said and then turned to Lyle. "Double time it. We aren't getting paid by the hour, and the sooner we're back aboard the *Rom*, the safer we'll all be."

The pod had the space to accommodate the doctor and wounded ensign, though it made for tight quarters. Lyle radioed the other pods to pass on Nicholson's orders to disengage from the hull of Atlantis Alpha and make for the surface at maximum speed.

Nicholson had to strap Waters into his seat as the ensign was too out of it to do anything more than stare up at him with dull, drug-glazed eyes. When he was done, Nicholson joined Lyle at the pod's controls.

"Mag-locks released," Lyle told him as Nicholson felt the pod drop loose into the water around the base. "Bringing engines online."

Nicholson smiled. Things could have gone a lot worse than they had. He was glad to be off Atlantis Alpha and headed for the *Rom.* He left the piloting to Lyle, twisting about in his seat to speak with Dr. Hydely who sat in the pod's rear next to Waters.

"You were in the process of explaining what happened here," Nicholson reminded him.

"There was recently a quake in the area," Hydely said. "It is my belief that the quake awoke a long-dormant lifeform never before encountered by man. That creature is responsible for the destruction of Atlantis Alpha."

Nicholson stared at the doctor and thought to himself, *So this is turning out to be a bad horror flick after all.*

"What sort of creature are we talking about, Dr. Hydely?" Nicholson asked.

"I can't really say," Dr. Hydely admitted. "I only caught a glimpse of it through the window of the base's command center before it struck the station. At that point, I was too busy trying to merely stay alive to give it much thought."

"Uh huh." Nicholson frowned. "That doesn't help very much."

"All I can tell you is that I believe it is some type of cephalopod."

"What the heck is a cephalopod?" Lyle asked without looking up from the pod's controls.

"He means a squid, don't you, Doctor?"

"Yes," Hydely answered. "That description is as good as any for the time being I suppose. Whatever it is, it is massive and far beyond anything on record…anywhere."

"That's just freaking great," Lyle laughed as his sarcastic nature came shining through.

"Do think the creature is still in the area?" Nicholson demanded, his thoughts fixed on the danger such a beast could represent to the pods under his command and the ships of DESRON 13.

Dr. Hydely shrugged. "There is simply no way to know that, Lieutenant. As I said, we are dealing with a completely unknown and never-encountered lifeform. It had perhaps vented its anger at being awakened by the quake on Atlantis Alpha and moved on, or it could very well be stalking us as prey at this very moment."

"Lyle, see if you can squeeze any more power out of the engines," Nicholson ordered. "I'll let Commodore Blanton know what we could be up against. In the meantime, Dr. Hydely, why don't you try to get some rest? I'm sure the commodore is going to have a lot more questions for you."

****

Commodore Blanton paced nervously about the bridge of the USS *Rom*. He couldn't shake the nervous energy that filled him.

The fact that he had heard from the pods he had dispatched and they were in route back to the ship was a relief, but the thought of some sort of monster out there, beneath the waves, that could be sizing up the DESRON under his command, was enough to put him on edge. Blanton was eager to meet Dr. Hydely face to face and hoped the doctor knew more than Lieutenant Nicholson had told him about the unknown threat they were dealing with.

Blanton could feel the eyes of his XO, Allen, on him. She was watching him like a hawk, waiting to see what else he did to respond to the danger they were in. He had already ordered all the ships in DESRON 13 to alert status. Their crews were at their battle stations and ready for action. They couldn't leave the area until the pods were back aboard, and that made them sitting ducks for whatever might be out there.

"Sir!" Blanton heard the *Rom*'s sonar tech, Glenn, shouted from his station. Both he and Allen started towards Glenn. Allen saw him and stopped, apparently not wanting to interfere with the actions of her superior officer. Blanton was glad for it.

Glenn looked over his shoulder at him with a confused expression as he moved to stand behind the sonar tech.

"What is it?" Blanton growled more gruffly than he had intended, putting on a thick air of authority for Allen's benefit.

"I don't know, sir." Glenn shrugged. "One second I thought I had a contact, the next, it was gone as if it was never there."

27

"We can't afford mistakes right now," Blanton firmly reminded Glenn. "What was it you thought you had on your screen that was troubling enough to call out like you did?"

"It was huge, sir. I mean really huge. Several times larger than this ship," Glenn babbled. "It was fast too. The flash of reading I got on it put the contact at doing over thirty knots."

"Biologic?" Blanton asked carefully.

"If you mean was it one of the genetically enhanced megalodons we were briefed on, sir, no, I don't think so. They're all supposed to have ID transponders in them, and I didn't pick up any kind of signal at all coming from the contact."

Blanton took a closer look at the screen in front of Glenn. "Whatever it was, it's certainly not showing up now."

"As I said, sir, it was just there and then gone." Glenn matched the snideness in Blanton's tone as he spoke this time.

"Stay on top of it," Blanton ordered. "If it shows again, I want to know about it. And you're sure it wasn't just your nerves getting the better of you?"

"No, sir," Glenn replied firmly.

Blanton turned away from Glenn without further comment. Allen moved to meet him as he headed for his command chair.

"That was a bit harsh." She grinned.

"We all need to stay alert right now," Blanton said, dismissing her concern. "A few harsh words now to keep him sharp are better than him screwing up down the road."

The grin vanished from Allen's expression. It was replaced by a stone cold one that implied to Blanton that she thought he had been the one who had screwed up, not Glenn.

"The pods are coming aboard now," she told him. "Should I have Dr. Hydely brought to the bridge?"

"No." Blanton took a seat in his chair. "Let's give the man a few minutes to get his crap together and realize he's safe now before we tear into him. Let our doctors do a work up on him, too. Lord only knows the stuff he was messing around with on that base. After that, send the good doctor to my ready room at oh sixteen hundred hours."

"Yes, sir." Allen nodded and left to carry out his orders.

****

Dr. Hydely was rather put out by all the poking and prodding the *Rom*'s medical staff put him through, despite his assurances to them that he wasn't a carrier of anything that could be a danger to the ship and her crew.

Nicholson and Lyle had been subjected to screenings as well, though on a far less intrusive level. They had already returned to active duty status. None the less, Nicholson had opted to remain in the medical bay with Hydely. He told himself it was so he would be there if the doctor decided to share anything else about the creature that had crushed Atlantis Alpha, but he had to wonder if he simply enjoyed watching the geeky little man's fits of self-righteous temper. Besides, he had nothing else better to do until the commodore or the ship's XO summoned him for a proper debriefing.

Hydely didn't seem to mind his presence. When the ship's medical staff finally released him, Hydely came swaggering straight up to him where he stood.

"Lieutenant, I would like to file a formal complaint about my treatment here," Hydely told him with anger burning in his eyes.

"Fine by me, Doc, but I'm just a grunt." He smirked. "You'll have to take that up either Commodore Blanton or the ship's XO."

Hydely's waterlogged clothes and lab coat were gone. They had been traded for a standard-issue Navy uniform. The doctor still carried all the papers and flash-drives he had saved from Atlantis Alpha, though. He had crammed them all in a combat backpack, stolen from Lyle, and refused to turn them over to the DESRON's techs for examination, claiming they were coded to erase themselves if handled by anyone other than himself. Commodore Blanton would surely be displeased with that, Nicholson figured, but for the time being, he wasn't going to tear them out of the doctor's clutches against his will. Hydely, himself, was the best source of information on Project Megalodons and the unknown creature out there anyway. Commodore Blanton would surely come to that conclusion too.

"Where is this Commodore Blanton you keep telling me about?" Hydely raged. "Doesn't he know that time is of the essence? That thing out there could strike at any moment!"

"Easy, Doc," Nicholson said. "Now that the folks here are willing to let you leave and you've checked out clean, I'll take you to him straightaway."

"It's about bloody well time," Hydely snapped and then shut up as the expression he wore shifted gears on a dime. "Look, Lieutenant Nicholson, I've been through a lot and perhaps am not coping with it all in the best of manner. I am deeply in your debt for saving my life and that of Ensign Waters. It's just that the danger to this DESRON is very real whether your commodore chooses to recognize that fact or not."

"It's okay, Doc," Nicholson said. "In your place, I'd be pretty rattled too. I get where you're coming from. Double check that you have everything you need in that backpack you stole from Lyle, and we'll get on our way to see the commodore, okay?"

"All my work is in here and safe, Lieutenant." Hydely raised the backpack so Nicholson could see it better. "Do please lead on then."

Nicholson led Dr. Hydely through the corridors and decks of the *Rom* to Blanton's ready room where the commodore already sat behind his desk waiting on them to arrive. Commodore Blanton rose from his seat as they entered.

"Lieutenant Nicholson." Blanton nodded at the sight of him then shifted his attention to Hydely. "Welcome aboard, Doctor. I'm sorry we couldn't meet under more pleasant circumstances. I've heard whispers about you and the work you're doing for some time now, and it has rather piqued my interest."

Blanton gestured at the two chairs in front of his desk. "Please take a seat, gentlemen, and let's get things sorted out, shall we?"

The commodore waited until the two of them got comfortable before he said anything more.

"Dr. Hydely, Lieutenant Nicholson has assured me that your creations from Project Megalodons had nothing to do with the attack on Atlantis Alpha, and that you claim an undersea quake has awoken some new type of monster, for lack of a better word, which may pose a threat to us all."

"That's correct, Commodore Blanton," the doctor began. "I believe our best hope of dealing with this—"

"Hold on a second, Doctor," Blanton cautioned Hydely. "We don't even know exactly what this monster is yet. I think that is where we need to begin."

Hydely, though appearing annoyed, paused to explain his beliefs about the monster that had been awakened. "What I can tell you about this new lifeform, Commodore, is that it is likely one of a kind and from an age long past. This creature has in all probability been lying dormant on the ocean floor since the ice age or before."

"That's a pretty big assumption to make, Doctor," Blanton challenged him.

"No, actually, it isn't," Hydely said. "I caught a glimpse of the monster as it attacked Atlantis Alpha, and I have seen its kind before or rather I have heard about them. There are legends about such creatures that stretch back to mankind's first voyages on the waves."

"So you do know what it is then?" Nicholson cut in.

"I suspect it is a Kraken, a creature straight out of myth." Dr. Hydely smiled. "What I saw and the brief look I got at the exterior damage to Atlantis Alpha I saw during our departure from the base both confirm this."

"And a Kraken is a giant squid?" Blanton leaned forward in this chair.

"A Kraken would be a cephalopod, yes, but I believe this one is of a species far more powerful than of the Krakens in mythology. Clearly, what it did to Atlantis Alpha proves the creature is not a threat to be taken lightly."

"I don't think anyone is taking all this lightly, Dr. Hydel." Blanton scowled.

"I suspect even the combined firepower of the entire DESRON under your command would have trouble stopping this Kraken. It is fast, massive, and uncannily strong. Beyond that, I believe it is intelligent as well."

"A thinking squid?" Blanton asked. Nicholson saw that Blanton was trying hard not to laugh in the doctor's face.

"I have no evidence to support my claim as of yet, Commodore Blanton. Call it a hunch, if you will, but I think it will prove a far more worthy opponent than you appear to be giving it credit for." Hydely scowled back at Blanton.

"Underestimating this thing is the worst mistake any of us could make."

"Trust me, Dr. Hydely, I shall remember that," Commodore Blanton assured him.

"What about DESRON 49?" Nicholson asked. "Do we even know where they are?"

"I have the exact coordinates for DESRON 49, assuming they haven't deviated from their orders," Dr. Hydely admitted.

"We will be needing those coordinates, Doctor," Blanton said. "Please deliver them to my XO, Allen, when our meeting here is done. Also, make sure she has the details for whatever frequency they have their comms tuned to. I don't give a rip how classified that info may be either. Give it to her. Do I make myself clear?"

"Completely," Hydely agreed.

"Lieutenant Nicholson, I want you to stay with the good doctor here at all times."

Nicholson opened his mouth to protest, but Commodore Blanton never gave him the chance.

"That's an order, Lieutenant. As long as the doctor is aboard this ship, his safety is your responsibility. See that he has whatever he needs to help provide us with more insight on this Kraken as well."

That was a dismissal if Nicholson had ever heard one, but Hydely stayed in his chair.

"Commodore," Hydely said, staring at Blanton, "it is imperative that you call in DESRON 49 and my megalodons at once. As I was attempting to say earlier, my megalodons are the best hope we have of combating the threat of the Kraken on equal terms."

"Lieutenant," was all Blanton said in reply before returning to the work he had been attending to when the two of them had entered.

"Come on, Doc," Nicholson urged, offering Hydely a hand up out of his chair. "It's time for us to go."

Hydely looked up at him and then back at Commodore Blanton before finally taking the offered hand and following him out of the room.

****

Captain Martin Flecker stared at the megalodon passing by the *Leary*. Flecker could tell that it was Curry by the long scar that stretched along the gigantic shark's back. The sense of fear and awe that Flecker felt being so close to any of Dr. Hydely's megalodons never diminished with time. Curry was almost as long as the *Leary*, coming in at a total length of four hundred and fifty feet from the tip of his snout to the end of his tail. Martin knew, too, that Hydely had somehow reinforced Curry's body structure and increased the shark's density to the point that if Curry wanted to, he could ram the *Leary* with enough force to fracture her hull and sink her.

Flecker wasn't an expert on normal sharks, much less these creatures that Dr. Hydely's work had brought into existence. He didn't know if there was an alpha in charge of all the others or not, but if there were, he would lay good money on it being Curry. He was the last of the creatures the doctor had given life to and his finest work. Flecker had seen Curry pull a sustained speed of above forty knots. It was hard to believe something so large could move so fast, but Flecker had seen it with his own eyes more than once.

All of Dr. Hydely's "improvements" in his megalodons weren't genetic or biological in nature. Flecker knew that some of them were cybernetic in nature, including the comm units embedded in each megalodon that allowed Dr. Hydely to control them. For this exercise, Flecker had been given access to a portion of the command codes that Hydely programmed the megalodons with. Flecker could talk to the megalodons in a sense, and that was perhaps the creepiest part of it all.

Based on his limited knowledge of how Hydely's implants in the megalodons worked, the implants didn't flat out control the megalodons as if the great sharks were robots, but rather imparted strong suggestions in the creatures' brains that pushed the megalodons to do certain things already within their nature. Those same implants somehow kept the megalodons from turning on the two destroyers and two frigates that made up the very strength of DESRON 49, which he commanded. He was glad that they did, though, or he and everyone in DESRON 49 would have been dead a long time back.

Flecker tore his attention away from watching Curry as the megalodon streaked on ahead of the *Leary* toward the horizon.

There were pressing matters he needed to attend to. Turning from the window of the ship's bridge, he returned to his command chair. His XO, Robbins, was waiting for him there.

"Those things are impressive, aren't they?" Robbins smiled.

"No doubt," Flecker agreed. "I am just glad they are on our side."

Flecker settled in his chair and looked over at Robbins who stood beside it. "Any word from Atlantis Alpha?"

"None," Robbins answered flatly.

"How long has it been now?" Flecker asked.

"Too long," Robbins assured him. "I strongly suggest we discontinue our planned exercises and return to the base. Those we left behind there may require our assistance."

"Anyone ever told you that you sound like a freaking Vulcan?" Flecker joked, though he was partly serious.

"Only you, sir." Robbins frowned.

"Okay, fine," Flecker relented. "Round up the megalodons and set us on a return course for Atlantis Alpha."

"As you say, sir." Robbins nodded and stepped away to carry out his orders.

Flecker had to admit that Robbins had a point. Atlantis Alpha hadn't responded to DESRON 49's mission updates in some time. The last communique the DESRON had received from the base had reported an undersea quake in the area of the base. Flecker doubted that such a quake could have seriously damaged a structure as hardened and reinforced at Atlantis Alpha, but it might have caused some disturbances that were playing havoc with the base's communication systems. At least he hoped that was all it was.

It would take about half an hour to get the megalodons all headed in the right direction, given that there were now two dozen of the great beasts under his command and each of them had their own distinct personalities and issues. Robbins would make it happen, though. There were times Flecker wanted to nickname his XO "the shark whisper," but he knew that Robbins would never get the joke, and he would just end having to explain it to the man in detail. Having a sense of humor was not something anyone who was a part of DESRON 49 ever thought of when they thought of Robbins.

"The *Peterson* is hailing us, sir," Flecker's comms officer informed him from her station.

"Patch 'em through, Diana," Flecker ordered. All things considered, he ran a very loose command despite his XO's ruthless quest for every t to be crossed and i dotted. Flecker liked addressing his crew by their first names and tended to make a habit of doing so.

"Flecker," Captain Peek's voiced boomed across the *Leary*'s bridge. "Why are you ordering us to head home? We're supposed to have another two weeks out here. We were just about to begin the most critical part of the tests Dr. Hydely ordered us to perform."

"Can't be helped, Kristen," Flecker sighed. "As you know, we haven't had any contact with Atlantis Alpha for some time now. We need to head back and find out what's going on at home."

"We've operated independently for far longer than this in the past, Flecker, and you know it. You're jumping the gun here and endangering the whole of Project Megalodons by doing this," Peek argued.

"I am fully aware of how important the results of these exercises are to the doctor's work, Captain," Flecker said, his voice firm and cold. "But this is my call to make, and you heard my orders."

"Yes, sir," Peek snarled. "I want it on record that I formally protest them, though."

"Done," Flecker told her.

"She's ended the transmission, sir," Diana told him.

Flecker gave Diana a nod of acknowledgment. "Thank you, Diana."

The trip back to Atlantis Alpha would take two days at normal speeds, but something inside Flecker told him that may be too long. Once the megalodons were rounded up and the DESRON got moving, he decided that he would shorten the trip as much as possible, even if it meant redlining the engines of the DESRON's ships. He toyed with the thought of sending the megalodons on ahead of the DESRON but thought better of it. The megalodons made up the bulk of DESRON 49's strength. If there was trouble ahead, he might need the great beasts with him when the crap hit the fan.

****

The glitches were getting worse. They weren't something Glenn could explain or even put his finger on exactly. There was just something *wrong* with the USS *Rom*'s sonar. He stared at the screen in front of him, trying to figure it out. He'd run every check he could think of and all the equipment was fine. The glitches were acting as if they were a product of an electromagnetic pulse, but there was no source for such a pulse to come from that Glenn knew of.

He leaned back in his chair, reaching for the cup of cold coffee next to his control board. He chugged half of it, hoping that it would kick his brain into high gear and give him some sudden insight to the problem with the sonar. It didn't. Glenn's cup crashed to the deck at his feet, shattering into pieces. The anomalous reading had returned and was CBDR on course towards DESRON 49. His instincts told him to yell for Allen's attention, as she currently had the conn while Commodore Blanton was absent from the bridge. He was terrified to do so, though. If the reading turned out to be nothing again, he was pretty sure the hammer would fall this time. He would be relieved from duty or worse. If he said nothing, on the other hand, the entire DESRON could be in danger. Just like before, the contact was reading as a massive entity moving at near impossible speed for its size.

Glenn ran the backside of his hand over his forehead. It came away wet. He discovered he was sweating despite the bridge's air conditioning. Swallowing hard, he decided he had to tell Allen about the contact.

"Ma'am!" he called to her. "The contact from earlier is back, and it's closing on us fast!"

"Speed and bearing?" Allen snapped, her attention suddenly solely focused on him.

"Close to forty knots, ma'am," Glenn told her. "It's subsurface and approaching from the west."

Allen had already moved to stand behind him, watching his screen over his shoulder herself.

"What in the devil is going on with the sonar, Glenn?" she asked.

She, too, had noticed the weird way the sonar data stream was cutting in and out.

"I honestly don't know, ma'am," Glenn admitted. "I'm working on it. So far, every part of the system I have checked has come up green and fully operational."

Allen dismissed the glitches, even though she had been the one to bring them up as the contact drew ever closer to DESRON 49. Relief washed over Glenn as she turned away from him, heading for the bridge's command chair, barking orders as she went.

"Officer Wedge, take the approaching contact with guns. Fire tubes one and two!"

"Yes, ma'am," Wedge blurted out, caught completely off guard by the need for action. He had been half-asleep in the chair and likely daydreaming of the future when this mission was over and done with.

"Taking contact with guns!" Wedge said as his fingers flew over the controls of his station. "Torpedoes are in the water."

The seconds ticked by like hours as everyone on the bridge waited with baited breath to see what happened when they reached the contact. Glenn watched them closing on his screen. Part of him hoped the approaching contact was nothing more than a sensor ghost. As the torpedoes struck the contact, he gave a muffled grunt. Whatever the contact was, it was real, and that was a very bad thing given its size, speed, and apparent hostile intent.

"Direct hits, ma'am!" Wedge informed Allen.

"Confirmed!" Glenn echoed the weapons officer.

"Contact status?" Allen demanded.

Glenn gaped at the data on his screen in disbelief. "Status unchanged. Unknown contact still closing at a speed of thirty-nine knots."

Allen slammed her fist on the arm of the command chair she sat in. "Alert the other ships of DESRON 49, and get Commodore Blanton up here, now!" she yelled.

"Ma'am, the contact has altered its course and heading to specifically target the *Sharp!*"

"Blast it!" Allen leaped up from her chair, standing in front of it. "Let Captain McKinney know trouble is headed his way. Have all other ships engage evasive maneuvers. Something tells me this contact isn't going to settle for just one of us, even if it manages to take out the *Sharp.*"

****

Captain McKinney's knuckles were white from the pressure of his grasp on the end of the arms of his command chair. His ship, the USS *Sharp,* was the most outlying of the DESRON 49's current formation. As the other ships of DESRON 49 began to break that formation to give him more room in which to maneuver and engage the inbound contact, he had ordered his helmsman to turn the *Sharp* so that she met the contact head on.

Alarm klaxons were blaring through the *Sharp* as McKinney yelled, "Hit that thing with everything we've got!"

His weapons officer scrambled to comply. Torpedoes fired from the ship's forward tubes as the *Sharp*'s missile launchers fired as well. Death came rushing towards the unknown contact from both above and below the waves. Ocean water sprayed into the air over the waves as the torpedoes and missiles reached their target and detonated. Traces of an oil-like liquid mingled with the water. McKinney hoped it was the blood of the contact the *Sharp* had just fired upon.

The *Sharp*'s C.I.W.S. triggered with a clap of thunder, nearly making McKinney wet himself. Fighting enemy ships was one thing, engaging an unknown hostile that very likely resembled some kind of creature straight out of a bad Sci-Fi flick was a whole other matter. Despite all of his years of experience, he was struggling to get a handle on the situation.

"Evasive maneuvers!" he shouted, knowing it was already too late for such an order. At the rate of speed the contact was traveling, there was just no hope of getting a ship as large as the *Sharp* out of the thing's path in time.

The contact rammed into the *Sharp*, the force of the impact actually lifting the forward deck of the destroyer up and out of the water. Metal shrieked, crumpling and folding inward along the length of her bow.

The bridge was in chaos. Damage and causality reports were coming in from all over the ship. Many of the crew on the bridge had been injured by the impact. One officer lay dead a few feet from where McKinney sat watching it all. The man had been tossed into one of the bridge walls at just the right angle to snap his neck. His head dangled at an unnatural angle atop his shoulders where his body rested, half-propped up, in the bridge's entrance door. Bright-red blood leaked from the corners of his mouth.

The helm had blown out from a power surge that raced through the *Sharp*'s systems at the moment of impact. The helm had erupted in an explosion of sparks and flames engulfing him. Another crewman managed to get the flames that burnt away at the helmsman's clothes and extinguished. The helmsman's flesh had sloughed away from the bones of his arms as the other officer tried to help the wounded helmsman to his feet. The helmsman screams of pain were as sickening as the sight of the exposed bones of his forearms.

McKinney's XO, Hall, was doing his best to restore order to the bridge as McKinney snapped into action. "Contact status?" he raged.

The sonar tech, Carle, was nursing a broken arm, though the man had managed to remain at his station. "Contact is coming about, sir!"

McKinney started to order his weapons officer to fire on the thing again but noticed the man was nowhere in sight. Dodging a piece of the bridge's ceiling as it crashed downward to clang against the deck, McKinney took over the weapons station himself. Most of the *Sharp*'s weapons were offline. He saw that the aft torpedo launchers were still functional. The contact had continued on past the ship after ramming it and was on its way back for another go at her. McKinney locked onto it and fired. One torpedo hit the water, speeding towards its intended the target. The other jammed inside its tube, detonating within it. The blast shook the *Sharp*, causing McKinney to lose his footing. He toppled, hard, onto the deck with a grunt of pain that took the breath from his lungs. Gasping for air, he grabbed hold of the weapons' console and used it to pull himself upright. He confirmed that the torpedo that had launched had struck the contact. The contact's course and speed, however, remained unchanged.

"Captain!" Carle shouted at him. "We have to abandon ship, sir! The *Sharp* is taking on more water than her pumps can handle, and nearly a third of the ship is on fire!"

"No!" McKinney yelled. "We can handle this! That thing out there has to be stopped before it goes after the rest of DESRON 49!"

Carle grabbed him and slammed up against the bridge wall.

"With what, sir?" Carle raged. "The ship is dead in the water. Most of her weapon systems are offline!"

McKinney struggled against Carle's hold on him. "We haven't lost this one yet! We can still…"

Carle's let go of him. McKinney staggered forward. He didn't see Carle's fist coming at him until it was too late. He heard the bone in his jaw crack and then he saw only darkness.

"Abandon ship!" Carle screamed at those around him, racing to the comm station to get the message out to the other survivors of the *Sharp*. "All hands! Abandon ship!"

****

Commodore Blanton had ordered the other ships of DESRON 49 not to engage the unknown contact that had targeted the *Sharp* unless it engaged them. A full-out battle at such close quarters could lead to friendly fire causalities on a large scale. He watched helplessly from the *Rom*'s bridge as the *Sharp* had been struck. The contact had then swung around to ram the ship a second time, breaking her to pieces. It all happened so fast that he doubted any of the *Sharp's* crew had been able to escape.

Immediately after tearing apart the *Sharp*, the contact had vanished. Glenn, his sonar tech, couldn't locate it, and Blanton was being told none of the other ships of the DESRON were having any luck doing so either. They were all reporting the same bizarre glitches in their sonar equipment that Glenn was dealing with aboard the *Rom.*

Blanton's instincts told him the creature, that was what the contact had to be, had dived towards the ocean floor. The tactic made sense. It kept the creature out of the DESRON's direct line of fire and gave it the initiative. Worse, it confirmed that the creature could *think* in tactical form or at least had the instincts for it. As fast and strong as the thing was, Blanton knew he was about to be in for the fight of his life. He hoped he was up to the challenge.

"Commodore! I've located the contact!" Glenn shouted. "It's underneath the *Bunn.*"

"Get me Captain Cullen!" Blanton snapped at his communications officer.

"Blanton!" Cullen's voice boomed over the comm. "That thing is under us!"

"I know," Blanton said. "Get out of there!"

"We can't!" Cullen told him. "It's got a hold on us somehow. The engines are already at half power and we're not moving. If we push any harder, the ship will be torn apart."

Suddenly, Cullen's voice was gone, and the open channel was filled with loud, crackling static.

Blanton moved to peer out of the *Rom's* forward window in the direction of the *Bunn.* Pure shock froze him in place as he saw what was happening to the *Bunn.* Impossibly long tentacles had risen from the water around the ship and wrapped about her. Gun emplacements exploded along her decks, crushed by the massive limbs. They didn't recoil even as the explosions spread, setting sections of the ship ablaze. Blanton could see the distant, tiny forms of the ship's crew throwing themselves from her decks in an effort to escape the horror that was engulfing the *Bunn.*

"Should we open fire, sir?" Allen asked, moving to stand at his side.

Blanton shook his head. "There are a lot of people on that ship, Allen."

"And there are a lot more on the *Rom,* the *Kirkman,* the *Stanz,* and the *Harrell,* too. What about them, sir?"

Blanton twisted his head to stare at her.

"If we don't take action now while that thing is an easy target, we may not get another chance like this again."

"I won't give that kind of order," Blanton said firmly. "We're not that desperate yet."

Allen frowned but let the argument go.

The tentacles around the *Bunn* constricted further. Blanton could see the ship's security personnel and marines on her deck pouring small arms fire vainly into the massive tentacles. A RPG struck one of the tentacles, blowing away a chunk of its flesh in a spray of black, oil-like blood. If the creature the limb belonged to felt any pain from the hit, there was no sign of it.

The pressure from the tentacles was beginning to take its toll on the hull of the ship. It began collapsing beneath the mighty limbs embracing it. The creature was crushing the ship slowly with its embrace. Blanton figured the *Bunn* didn't have much time left until something truly vital gave inside her structure and the end came.

Without warning, the tentacles holding the *Bunn* yanked her downwards into the water. Blanton's eyes bugged at the sight. The creature had just pulled a full-sized destroyer beneath the waves. The *Bunn* was gone.

"God in heaven help us," he heard Allen mutter.

"Amen," Blanton whispered too low for her to hear in reply.

****

"Get the DESRON out of here!" Blanton ordered. "Maximum military speed!"

The remaining ships of DESRON 49 were pouring it on to in an attempt to make a break for it while the creature that had just dragged the *Bunn* to a watery grave was hopefully still busy with her. Blanton's own ship, the *Rom,* was in the lead. Every ship of DESRON 49 was moving at thirty knots or more except for the *Kirkman*. She was pulling around twenty-eight knots. Something had blown in her main engine, and according to the reports coming in, it was the best she could manage. Repairs were being worked on, but Blanton knew they wouldn't be completed in time. He was now faced with the choice of leaving the *Kirkman* behind to fend for itself or ordering all the ships of DESRON 49 to form up and make a stand against the creature, here and now. Blanton wanted to fight. He really did. He wanted to see the water turn black with the monster's blood, but he knew that, for now, the creature had the upper hand. They knew too little about it, and it had just proven how deadly it was. If he ordered the ships of the DESRON to come about and engage it, that thing out there might win the day. It was a chance he couldn't afford to gamble on. DESRON 13 and Dr. Hydely's creations were still out there somewhere. DESRON 49's best hope was to locate and join up with them. Their combined forces and more time to figure out how to effectively battle the creature would, he believed, better their chances of victory.

Blanton forced himself to sit down in his command chair. His heart was pounding in his chest and adrenaline was pumping through his system. He was keenly aware of each passing second as DESRON 49 fled. Three minutes had passed with no sign of the creature. He knew this fight wasn't over yet, though. The *Kirkman* kept falling further and further behind. Her captain, Wightman, had been trying to contact him, but Blanton had allowed his communications officer to deal with her so far. He couldn't do that much longer. He needed to man up and just tell Wightman that she was going to be on her own.

Gesturing to his comms officer to patch Wightman through, Blanton sighed. Telling someone they were about to take one for the greater good and likely die in the process was one of the worst parts of command.

"Commodore Blanton," Wightman started, but he cut her off.

"Captain Wightman, I'm sorry," he said with sadness in his voice. "I'm sorry, but we have no choice but to leave you behind."

"That's a coward's move, and you know it, Blanton!" Wightman raged at him.

"I'm sending over coordinates now for a rallying point. I hope to see you there," Blanton told her and then signaled for his comms officer to end the transmission.

Wightman was still yelling at him until the channel closed, and her voice abruptly went silent.

Blanton rubbed at his temples and looked up at his XO, Allen, ready for another outburst from her as well. It never came, though. Allen met his gaze and said, "You did the right thing, Commodore."

"Doesn't make it any easier," he said.

"It never does," Allen agreed.

****

A litany of curses that would have made even the crudest of sailors blush erupted from Captain Maria Wightman as Commodore Blanton had cut her off. That bastard was just going to leave her and her crew aboard the *Kirkman* behind, and there was nothing she could do about it. As she began to get control of her anger and calm down, she saw the expressions on the faces of her bridge crew. They looked more terrified of her than the fact that they had just been left to die by the rest of DESRON 49.

"Maintain battle stations," she ordered then focused her gaze on Larson, her sonar tech. "Any sign of that thing out there?"

"Not yet, ma'am, but that same, strange interference is still playing havoc with the sonar systems."

"Mr. Ovard," Wightman turned to her weapons officer, "I want options on how best to stop that creature when it shows itself, and I want them now."

Ovard looked as if he wanted to make a run for it but somehow managed to stay at his station. "Ma'am, so far nothing that DESRON 49 has done has even slowed that thing out there down."

"Don't you think I know that, Ovard?" Wightman roared. "That's why I am asking you to come up with something better, blast it!"

"Yes, ma'am," Ovard nodded, looking paler than usual. "We've seen plenty of evidence that the thing out there can be hurt, Captain, we just haven't been able to hurt it enough at once to have our fire really matter... Or at least, I hope that's the case. I recommend engaging it from as far a distance out as we can and hitting it with everything we can throw its way in a sustained barrage. If we are lucky, the cumulative damage might take its toll on the monster."

"We may not have the option of engaging it from a distance," Wightman pointed out. "You did just see what the thing did to the *Bunn*, didn't you?"

"Yes, ma'am," Ovard stammered, "I did. If it gets the drop on us like that, odds are our only hope of doing that thing any real damage is to blow the ship ourselves while it has a hold on us."

Wightman fought not to fly off the handle again, biting her tongue until she got control of her emotions. "That's not an option, Mr. Ovard. My duty is to get this ship and her crew out of here, not destroy her myself while killing us all in the process."

"Contact approaching from aft!" Larson's panicked cry rang out. "CBDR, speed—forty knots! Impact in three minutes!"

"Well, Mr. Ovard," Wightman gritted her teeth, "you better come up with something and fast. Take that thing with guns and show it we have some teeth too!"

As Ovard began targeting the creature, Wightman turned her fury upon the *Kirkman's* helmsman. Scott flinched as she shouted at him, "Get us more speed! We need every second we can get!"

"Yes, ma'am," Scott answered, desperately trying to see if engineering could wrangle any more power out of the engines.

The *Kirkman's* modified C.I.W.S. came alive spraying rounds at the approaching creature at a rate of three thousand a minute. Ovard opened up on the thing with everything he had at his disposal. He emptied the aft torpedo tubes at the creature and sent a volley of missiles descending upon its location as well. The water churned and flew skyward as the torpedoes and missiles hammered the monster. The water flushed black at the point of contact where the barrage met the creature.

"Direct hits on all counts!" Larson yelled. "Contact is breaking off!"

Wightman slumped into her chair, stunned. She hadn't expected that even throwing everything they had the creature would work but it had…at least for the moment.

"Captain!" Scott called, snapping her from her thoughts. "Engineering has been able to slightly increase power to the engines. I've been able to bring our speed up to thirty knots!"

Again, the unexpected good news was like a bucket of cold water thrown into her face. Wightman was actually beginning to allow herself to hope that she and her crew might make it through this mess.

"The contact has come about and altered its course again!" Larson said. "CBDR on our port side! Closing at…" the sonar tech paused, sucking in a sharp breath, "forty-two knots, Captain!"

"I think we just ticked that thing off for real," Ovard said.

"Impact in less than two minutes!" Larson wailed.

"Mr. Ovard," Wightman started.

"Already on it, ma'am," Ovard assured her.

The ship's C.I.W.S. whirred around on its turret to engage the approaching monster. Ovard didn't have a direct line of fire with any of the *Kirkman*'s torpedoes this time. He had to rely entirely on the ship's missile systems and side gun emplacements. Those emplacements opened fire as the crews manning them did what they could to hurt the approaching monster. Most of the missile launchers had been emptied in Ovard's first attack on the creature, leaving only a handful of missiles to streak outward over the water towards the monster. They dove downward as they reached the creature's location, plunging into the depths to meet it there.

The exploding missiles flung black-tinted water into the air. This time, though, they simply weren't enough, even combined with the fire of the ship's gun emplacements and C.I.W.S. The creature swam onward towards the *Kirkman*, increasing speed as it came.

"Contact is now closing at forty-four knots!" Larson shouted.

Before the sonar tech could say anything else, the creature plowed into the *Kirkman*. It struck the middle of the ship like an impossibly large torpedo, breaking the ship in half. Stations blew out all over the bridge as men and women screamed in a mixture of pain and terror. The bridge's ceiling collapsed in a rain of fragmented metal that impaled more than one of Wightman's personnel. Even Wightman didn't escape uninjured as the bridge floor bucked and sent her toppling from her command chair. She hit the floor, face first, and tasted blood. Pushing herself up with her arms, she spat red-slicked teeth.

Both Ovard and Larson were dead. Ovard's skull had been crushed when the ceiling came down, and Larson sat twisted about in his chair with a piece of glass from the sonar screen protruding from the center of his throat. Rivers of red flowed over the front of Larson's uniform from the clearly lethal wound.

Wightman felt hands taking hold of her and helping her to her feet. They belonged to her XO. McMillian took the brunt of most of her weight as the muscles of Wightman's leg seemed to refuse to work. She realized with a start that she couldn't feel them. Wightman glanced down at the mangled meat that used to be her legs and promptly threw up in McMillian's arms.

She could hear McMillian screaming at her for orders, but his voice sounded miles away, drowned out by the ringing in her ears. It was when she saw the wave of ocean water smash in the bridge's forward window as it came rushing towards her and McMillian that she knew it was all over.

****

"The *Kirkman* is gone, sir," Glenn informed Commodore Blanton.

The *Rom,* the *Stanz*, and the *Harrell* were all that remained of DESRON 49. In next to no time at all, the creature had taken half of the ships under Blanton's command out of play. It seemed surreal. Blanton shuddered as his mind tried to process the reality of it all.

"And the creature?" Blanton asked.

Another voice spoke from behind where he sat in his command chair. He recognized it as belonging to Dr. Hydely.

"Call it a Kraken, Commodore Blanton, because that is what it is," the doctor said. He and Lieutenant Nicholson had slipped onto the bridge without Blanton noticing.

Blanton ignored him. "Report!" he snapped at Glenn.

"The creature...er...the Kraken is either out of the current limited range of our sonar, sir, or she's gone deep again," Glenn answered.

Blanton whirled on Dr. Hydely and Nicholson. "How long have you two been here?"

"Long enough to see that Captain Wightman hurt that Kraken, or whatever you want to call it, pretty good before it broke the *Kirkman* apart." Nicholson moved closer to Blanton's command chair. "I think she may have just bought us some time."

"I agree," Dr. Hydely chimed in. "That thing has been asleep for a very long time. I highly doubt it expected to be hurt in such a manner by things the size of your ships, Commodore."

"How can you be sure of that, Doctor?" Blanton challenged Hydely.

"I can't. Call it a gut feeling if you will, but I do believe it will take at least some time to nurse its wounds before it makes another run at this DESRON." Hydely's tone was matter of fact and perhaps even a touch detached as if he were safe in a lab talking about a specimen he was working on.

"Half a DESRON," Blanton snarled.

"None the less," Allen jumped into the conversation before Blanton could turn too morbid about the situation. "If we do have some time, we had best use it to do something to even the odds before that Kraken decides to come calling again."

The course of the remaining ships of DESRON 49 was set for the coordinates that Hydely had given them in regards to DESRON 13's likely location.

"Increase our speed beyond the redline," Blanton ordered. "Have the *Stanz* and the *Harold* do the same. Finding DESRON 13 may be our only hope. In the meantime, Hydely, Nicholson, you two join me in my ready room. Ms. Allen, you have command."

"Yes, sir," Allen barked, slipping into his chair as Blanton got out of it.

Hydely and Nicholson followed him from the bridge. When they reached his ready room, Blanton gestured for them to take the empty chairs in front of his desk, and he clawed open the desk's side drawer to produce a bottle of Vodka and three glasses. He filled each, passing a glass to both the doctor and Nicholson.

Blanton slammed his down his throat with a jerk of his head, enjoying the burn as the liquid flowed into him, before he took his own seat.

Nicholson had drained his glass as well, but Hydely held his as if it were a vial of deadly poison. Hydely leaned forward to place the still-full glass atop Blanton's desk as the commodore stared at him.

"I don't drink," Hydely said, his cheeks red. "Health issues, I am afraid. Thank you, though."

"Doctor," Blanton tried to keep the anger within in check as he spoke, "that Kraken just took out three state-of-the-art United States' destroyers with what appeared to be very little effort on its part. If there is anything, anything at all, you can tell us about how to stop that monster, I need to know it now."

Hydely shrugged. "It's just flesh and blood, Commodore. Shoot it enough, and it will die."

"That's not very helpful, Doctor." Blanton's lips curled into a frown.

"I know a way to stop it," Nicholson admitted.

"Oh, is that so, Lieutenant?" Blanton asked, making his doubt clear in the tone of his voice.

"Lure it in and allow it to grapple one of our remaining ships," Nicholson suggested. "When it does, we blow that ship in its arms like a bomb."

"That could work!" Hydely said excitedly.

Blanton wanted to throttle them both. Did they really expect him to ask one the crews under his command to give their lives to stop that thing out there?

"I am not ready to do that, Lieutenant," Blanton growled. "I agree that what you have suggested just might work, but at this point, it's too high a price to pay."

"If the lieutenant's idea is too high a price as you say, then my megalodons are your only hope, Commodore," Hydely told him. "I created them to be the apex predators of the oceans. They have a far better chance of stopping the Kraken than any of your ships do."

"That's great, Doctor," Blanton mocked Hydely, "but we still haven't located them or DESRON 13 yet, and there is no guarantee that we will before the Kraken returns."

"Then, Commodore Blanton," Hydely replied in a smug voice, "I suggest you either go with the lieutenant here's plan, or start praying really hard that we do reach DESRON 13 in time."

****

Captain Flecker, aboard the USS *Leary,* the flagship of the understrength DESRON 13, was utterly surprised when his XO, Robbins, informed him that long-range radar had picked up three naval vessels approaching their formation from the north.

"Who in the devil are they?" Flecker asked Robbins.

"Best guess, sir? I would wager they were dispatched to investigate the lack of communication with Atlantis Alpha just as we are heading back to do ourselves," Robbins ventured.

"But why only three ships?" Flecker questioned. "That just doesn't make sense. One would think they would have sent a full strength DESRON given Atlantis Alpha's level of importance."

"I couldn't say, sir." Robbins shrugged. "I highly recommend we make contact with them at once to determine their purpose and intent."

"Our orders—" Flecker said.

"I am well aware of the restrictions placed upon us by Dr. Hydely and Atlantis Alpha, sir," Robbins reminded him. "None the less, making contact with those ships is our best move at this time. They could process information about the lack of contact with Atlantis Alpha that we sorely need."

"Make it so then." Flecker nodded at his communications officer.

Diana nodded back at him and began opening a channel to the distant ships. "This is the USS *Leary* in command of the United States' DESRON 13. Please identify yourselves or you will be fired upon."

Robbins' eyes bugged in their sockets, and he started towards Diana, but Flecker stopped him, holding him in place by putting a hand on his chest.

"I approve the liberties Diana just took with that message, Robbins," he said. "There are three destroyers out there. It's better for us to sound strong than weak if for some reason they are hostile."

Flecker could see a vein throbbing on the side of Robbins' forehead, but the XO kept his mouth shut and deferred to Flecker's judgment.

"As you say, sir," Robbins answered.

"Sir," Diana called for their attention. "The approaching vessels identify themselves as the remnants of DESRON 49."

"Remnants?" Flecker repeated the word.

"Yes, sir," Diana confirmed. "They claim that Atlantis Alpha was attacked and destroyed by some sort of monster awakened by the quake in its area. They say they engaged the creature while in route to us and have taken heavy losses."

"Did they say what kind of creature?" Robbins asked.

"They're calling it a Kraken, sir." Diana's eyes were wide.

"Hard to believe Atlantis Alpha is lost," Flecker admitted. "I've been down there. It was one bloody tough base."

"Commodore Blanton of DESRON 49 also reports that they have Dr. Hydely with them aboard their flagship," Diana continued.

"Well, thank God for that," Flecker exclaimed. "That weirdo can have his sharks back."

Flecker noticed Robbins shoot him a sharp glance at his rather unprofessional comment.

"What?" Flecker laughed. "Those megalodons creep me out and you know it."

Robbins raised an eyebrow at his reply but said nothing more.

"Change our course to intercept DESRON 49's and bring us in to join their formation. I imagine this Commodore Blanton and I have a lot we need to discuss."

****

Commodore Blanton would have greatly preferred the meeting with Captain Flecker and his XO to have taken place aboard the *Rom.* He had every right to require it. He outranked Flecker and had added the ships of DESRON 13 to his command. He was glad for the additional firepower the two destroyers and two frigates added to his own. Dr. Hydely had insisted the meeting take place aboard Flecker's ship, the *Leary*, however. Hydely claimed the *Leary* would be the key to combating the Kraken that was out there somewhere, stalking them. The *Leary* was equipped with all the gear that Dr. Hydely needed to control his pet megalodons and use them against the great beast. Blanton had given into the doctor's request as he couldn't argue that the megalodons could make the difference in whether or not all them made it home or ended up in watery graves.

Leaving the *Rom* under Allen's command, Blanton, Lieutenant Nicholson, and Dr. Hydely, accompanied by a detachment of armed marines, had risked the trip over to the *Leary*. They had reached the ship and came aboard safely to find Flecker and his XO, Robbins, waiting on them. They were quickly led to a conference room just off the *Leary*'s bridge.

Everyone took their seats, with Captain Flecker allowing Blanton to take the seat at the head of the table in respect to Blanton's rank. Blanton saw quickly that Flecker was a very loose type of captain and didn't always play things by the book. Flecker was several years younger than he was. His intense blue eyes rested below a mop of poorly combed brown hair.

"Glad to have you aboard, Commodore Blanton, sir," Flecker said. "I wish it was under less dire circumstances."

"Drop the small talk, Captain," Blanton ordered. "We have no time for it. There's a monster out there that just destroyed three of my ships. Dr. Hydely tells me that he can use the megalodons you have with you to stop it."

Flecker smiled. "Did you catch a glimpse of them as you were coming aboard?"

Blanton nodded. "I did. They look very…aggressive."

"That might just be the understatement of the eon, sir," Flecker chuckled. "I have to admit I am rather glad Dr. Hydely is here. I am more than ready to pass them back into his hands."

"How has the behavior of my megalodons been, Captain Flecker?" Hydely inquired.

"They are fine, Doctor." Flecker grinned. "I mean, for strong-willed killing machines. Sometimes, we have a bit of trouble getting them to carry through with their orders, but if you're asking if they've turned on us in some form, the answer is no."

"Good." Hydely smiled at Flecker. "Commodore Blanton, I would like to leave this meeting at once to personally check on my creations and began preparations for the battle that surely lies ahead of us. Captain Flecker is more than aware of the megalodons' capabilities and can answer any questions you might have in that regard."

"Permission granted, Doctor." Blanton gestured at Nicholson. "Go with him, Lieutenant, and make sure he stays out of trouble."

"Yes, sir," Lieutenant Nicholson answered, leaving his seat to follow Dr. Hydely out of the conference room.

"Now, gentlemen," Blanton leaned forward in his seat, placing his hands on the top of the table, "let's get down to business. Exactly how many megalodons are with you, Captain Flecker?"

"I am sure you're aware that information is classified, sir," Flecker said but quickly caved beneath Blanton's glaring stare. "Two dozen, sir, all combat ready."

"And Dr. Hydely controls these megalodons via implants he embedded in them?" Blanton asked.

It was Flecker's XO, Robbins, who answered this time. "Yes. Not all of Dr. Hydely's work with the sharks was biological in nature. There are certain cybernetic elements to his work as well."

"I see," Blanton commented. "This Kraken out there, I believe, emits some type of electromagnetic pulse. Whether the pulse is an intentionally used weapon against us or merely a natural function of the creature's biology doesn't matter. It has caused numerous problems with our sonar and radar equipment. Should I be concerned that it might affect these implants the doctor uses to control the megalodons are well?"

Flecker seemed to think over the question before responding. "I don't think so, Commodore. Hydely's work is years ahead of anything else I have ever encountered, and the implants are shielded against EMP attacks." Flecker spread his hands wide.

"The doctor likes to cover his bases. He's spent the better part of his life making the sharks of Project Megalodons as unstoppable by conventional means as he could. You mentioned that the pulse from the Kraken didn't affect all the systems of your ships like the EMP from a nuke detonation would have. Therefore, I just don't know how it would be possible for such a low-level pulse to interfere with the doctor's control of the megalodons at all."

"Good to know." Blanton allowed himself a smile. "We won't truly know until the sharks have directly engaged the Kraken on our behalf, but I'll take your word that the odds are in our favor."

"I had the chance to read the reports you sent over about your engagement with the Kraken, Commodore Blanton," Robbins spoke up. "The amount of fire you claim your ships poured into the beast with little or no effect is staggering. Just how tough is this Kraken?"

"We don't have any idea of its real strength, gentlemen, but I can tell you it's fast enough to outrace any of us at top speed, smart enough to know exactly when and how to hit us for maximum effect, and strong enough to crush a ship like it was soda can if it gets its tentacles around it."

Blanton didn't blame Flecker and Robbins for disbelieving him and he could see that they did by their expressions. Yesterday, he wouldn't have believed such a story himself.

"I am sure the doctor's megalodons can handle it, sir," Robbins assured him.

"I suppose we'll find out," Blanton commented.

****

Lieutenant Nicholson watched Dr. Hydely racing from one console to another with an expression of a kid in a candy store. The doctor was excited to have a real means of testing the combat viability of his megalodons against the Kraken. Nicholson knew that Hydely had run numerous sims and actual real world exercises with his megalodons, but they were nothing like the battle that the giant sharks were about to head into.

"Doc, are you sure your sharks are up for this?" Nicholson asked.

"Oh, they are ready, Lieutenant." Hydely paused in his path from a terminal that displayed the vital signs of the various sharks and one that appeared to their main control console. "This will be a perfect test for them, better than anything I could have arranged myself. The universe has been very kind to us today indeed."

Nicholson shook his head. "I've been around you long enough now to know what you mean, but you better watch that kind of talk with Commodore Blanton and the others. We've lost an entire base and three destroyers so far to this Kraken thing. Slow down for a minute and think about that. I mean about how many good men and women have died already because of that monster out there."

Hydely appeared to try to stop smiling and failed miserably. "I am aware of the price your fellows have paid, Lieutenant.

However, once my megalodons have been properly bloodied, I want you to imagine how many lives will be saved by them taking the place of ships such as this one. War on the waves will never be the same, and we will have the upper hand."

Nicholson sighed seeing that Dr. Hydely just didn't get it. The doctor was too lost in his work. "If you say so, Doc." Nicholson gestured at the room full of equipment. "Anything I can do to help?"

"You're doing it already, Lieutenant, by staying out of my way." Dr. Hydely grinned.

Finally, Hydely seemed to have everything in order as he needed it. He took a seat in the center of the room and lifted a bizarre helmet onto his head. "Plug me in if you would, Lieutenant."

Nicholson moved to take the end of the cable Hydely held out to him and plugged it into the massive computer system behind where the doctor sat.

Hydely went stiff in his chair as if his body was being raked by an electrical current that locked his muscles in place. Just as suddenly, he relaxed. Hydely raised his right hand to touch the side of the helmet he wore. "I'm a part of them now, Lieutenant. Everything they see and feel, I experience as well. The megalodons and I are two made one in a sense."

Nicholson wondered just how crazy Hydely really was. The doctor looked as if he were high and floating on cloud nine.

"What's it like?" Nicholson asked.

"There are no words to describe it, Lieutenant Nicholson. Even as I listen to your words, I am swimming through the depths."

"Uh huh," Nicholson grunted.

Hydely's expression changed instantly. "My megalodons..." he croaked. "They're afraid."

"Of the Kraken?"

"Yes," Hydely answered in a voice no louder than a whisper. "The Kraken is coming. They can feel it closing in on us. I can feel it too. It's like a great mass of darkness eating the rising sun of a new day."

Nicholson didn't have a freaking clue what Hydely meant by that, but he wasn't about to ask.

"I am dispatching six of my children to engage it while it is still far distant from our current position. Please inform your commodore of this."

"Sure thing," Nicholson said, nodding. He walked over to a comms panel on the room's wall and stabbed the button to activate it with his thumb.

"Patch me through to Commodore Blanton's current location," he ordered.

A few seconds later, Blanton's voice came over the comm. "What is it, Lieutenant?"

"Dr. Hydely wishes that I inform you of the fact that he has just dispatched one-fourth of the megalodon force accompanying us to engage the Kraken."

"He did what?" Blanton roared.

Nicholson repeated himself.

"He has no authorization to do such a thing!" Blanton fumed. "Have him call those megalodons back at once."

"I don't know that I can, sir," Nicholson said honestly. "The tech he's using down here is way beyond anything I've ever dealt with before. If I just disconnect the doctor, I don't know what it will do to him or the sharks, sir."

"Disconnect him?"

"Yes, sir," Nicholson confirmed. "The doctor has initiated what I assume is a direct mental link with the megalodons. Their minds are interfaced on a very deep and intimate level. As I said, just yanking him out of it against his will might have some rather unpleasant consequences for both Hydely and the sharks."

"I see," Commodore Blanton said and then paused. Nicholson could hear him consulting with Captain Flecker. "Leave the doctor be for right now then. Watch him closely, though, and contact us at once if things go pear-shaped down there."

"Understood and will do, sir," Nicholson confirmed.

****

The six megalodons sped through the water. Their massive bodies glided along at a speed close to thirty knots. Dr. Hydely was with them inside their minds, urging them onward. He could feel the water flowing over their skin as they swam. He could feel the coolness of the water around them. He also felt the megalodon's abating fear. When they had first sensed the

70

Kraken, something primordial had been triggered within them much like a powerful survival instinct that told them to flee. Their training and the alterations that Hydely had made to them genetically, though, quickly began to combat that fear and now had reduced it to nothing more than a determined apprehension.

Hydely had known the Kraken emitted a low-level EMP. It manifested through his link with the megalodons as a dull, throbbing pain in his temples beneath the helmet his body wore back aboard the USS *Leary*. It grew stronger with each passing second as the megalodons closed on their prey. The Kraken was well aware of the megalodons' presence and intent. It didn't appear threatened by the approaching megalodons at all. It kept its own course, coming onwards towards them at ramming speed.

The megalodons were close enough to the Kraken now that Hydely released them from his control, allowing the great sharks to make their own decisions tactically in terms of how to engage the Kraken. Their judgment in such matters was far superior to his, and he trusted them to be able to handle the Kraken. Hydely rode along in the back of the megalodons' minds as a silent passenger still plugged into their senses and emotions. Thus far, his focus had been on the megalodons themselves. He hadn't bothered to truly study the seeming force of nature they were up against. He did so now and nearly disconnected from the minds of the great sharks from the shock of what he saw through their eyes. The Kraken's central mass alone was several times that of the largest destroyer in DESRON 49, and its tentacles seemed to stretch onward, away from its body, for miles. With a start, he realized why his sharks had initially felt terror when they sensed the monster. The Kraken was a creature from the darkest nightmares of the deep.

The six megalodons broke formation as they increased their speed to upwards of thirty-two knots. They spread out on their approach, each of them taking a different route towards the moving mountain of sheer tentacled power ahead of them. Hydely recognized that the sharks were hoping that some of them might make it through the Kraken's defending tentacles this way to get a shot at the creature's central mass. It was clear they were willing to take losses to achieve this because there was no hope of all of them escaping the limbs that sprang forward to meet them.

One tentacle lashed out at an approaching megalodon. It whipped the great shark's side, slashing its flesh to draw first blood. The force of the blow sent the megalodon spinning away through the water. Another tentacle snaked its way around a second megalodon with impossible speed. The megalodon never stood a chance. The tentacle tightened about the shark, pulling its body underneath the pressure of its grip. A third tentacle shot outward, but this time, the megalodon it was aiming for was ready. It caught the tentacle in its mouth, its razor teeth sinking into the flesh they closed upon. Black blood seeped from the wound and the sides of the megalodon's mouth. The great shark and the tentacle wrestled in the water as it churned about them.

At last, the tentacle ripped free of the megalodon's hold, leaving a chunk of itself protruding from the shark's mouth.

And so the battle raged. Red and black blood mingled in the salty ocean waters. Another megalodon died as a tentacle entered its body through its wide open mouth and tore its way along the shark's throat and through its entire form for its tip to emerge through the shark's back.

Two of the megalodons, dodging and rolling in the water, escaped the clutches of the Kraken's tentacles to reach the giant monster's central mass. They plowed into it, their teeth biting and shredding the flesh of the Kraken where they met it. Then the Kraken itself rolled in the water, its massive body turning end over end as it freed itself from the two sharks that had managed to close on it. Its tentacles recoiled, drawing up close to the monster's central mass. Hydely sensed that the sharks knew what the Kraken was about to do and desperately tried to flee. They turned tail, pouring on speed, but it wasn't enough. The Kraken's tentacles all exploded outward at once, striking like thrusting swords. The two megalodons closest to the monster were gutted and impaled upon them.

With four of the megalodons dead and a fifth wounded, Hydely struggled to regain control of the surviving sharks. Their minds fought his. It took all the effort he could muster to push his way in to the point of controlling them. Their fear was thick and like a tangible wall he had to batter over and over until he finally smashed into the control centers of their minds. He sent the unwounded shark racing back towards DESRON 49. The wounded one, he did his best to override the pain centers of its brain to give the shark what clarity of thought that he could. It had been badly hurt, and Hydely was surprised it could move at all once he understood just how badly. Much of its skeletal structure had been shattered by the blow the Kraken had dealt it. It was weak from blood loss as well. Currents of red still leaked from its open side as it tried to flee the Kraken under Hydely's urging and desperate command.

Wounded as it was, the megalodon was simply too slow. Two of the Kraken's tentacles closed upon it. The megalodon whipped its tail and fought hard against their hold but to no avail. The hold of the tentacles only grew tighter upon its body. With a single yank in opposite directions, the two tentacles tore the megalodon apart. Entrails spilled from its two halves into the water.

With a scream, Hydely lost his connection with the sharks and awoke on the *Leary*. His skin was slicked with sweat that ran over the curves of his skin to drip onto the floor. His eyes were bloodshot and half mad as his hands clutched the helmet he wore to fling it across the room. It clanged into the room's far wall before bouncing onto the floor.

****

Lieutenant Nicholson had been on the verge of panic as Dr. Hydely's condition beneath the helmet he wore had grown worse and worse. It was like watching someone face death in slow motion. Hydely had started to sweat first. His muscles began to spasm as the doctor's body had rocked about in the chair he sat in. The tiniest drops of blood were beginning to leak from the corners of his eyes and his ears. Every so often, his entire body jerked about as if something had struck it with great force. When Hydely awoke, ripping off the helmet, Nicholson had almost cried out in relief. If the doctor hadn't been able to break free from whatever was happening to him, Nicholson knew he would have to have taken measures that likely would have stood as much chance of killing the doctor or leaving him brain-dead as they did for freeing him.

Nicholson rushed to Hydely, catching the doctor as he half-leaped, half-fell from his chair. Hydely looked at him with weak and sunken eyes as if Hydely had no idea who he was or even where he was.

"You okay, Doc?" Nicholson asked.

"My megalodons…" Hydely stammered. "They're dead."

Nicholson helped Hydely stand upright, supporting most of the doctor's weight himself.

"Looks like you had a pretty close call there yourself, Doc," Nicholson said, feigning a laugh. "And one of the group you sent did get away."

"The Kraken!" Hydely suddenly shouted, ignoring the soldier's words and regaining his strength to pull out of Nicholson's hold on him. "It's coming!"

"We know, Doc," Nicholson assured him. "We know. We picked up the monster on sonar no longer after you took your megs to stop it."

"It killed them all," Hydely muttered as tears well up in his eyes. "They barely managed to hurt it."

"Don't worry, Doc," Nicholson said, trying to stay positive. "You still got eighteen more."

Hydely shook his head. "You don't understand. I was there for it all. I felt each and every one of them die."

"I think you need some rest, Doc," Nicholson urged. "Let me help you to the med bay."

"No," Hydely protested. "The Kraken is coming. Didn't you hear me?"

"Commodore Blanton and Captain Flecker will deal with it. You can barely stand up, man. What exactly do you think you're going to be able to stop that monster?"

"Other than Flecker, I am the only one who can interface with the megalodons. You need me, Lieutenant. Flecker doesn't have the experience with the mental merger with the sharks that I do. If you want to live, you have to let me stay here and fight that thing again."

"That's not up to me, Doc," Nicholson admitted. "My job is to keep an eye on you and make sure you don't get yourself killed."

Hydely had placed a hand atop the chair he had been sitting in to steady himself. Even so, Nicholson could see it was all the doc could do to just stay on his feet.

"We've gotten along well so far, Doc, but don't push me on this one," Nicholson warned him. "I'm taking you to medical. If you want to do it the hard way, that's up to you, but we're going one way or the other."

For a moment, Nicholson actually thought Hydely was going to take a swing at him. Thankfully, the doctor didn't. Instead, he nodded.

"I suppose you're right, Lieutenant," Hydely croaked. "You may have to carry me, though."

And with that, Hydely toppled over onto the floor to land with a thud at Nicholson's feet, the last of his strength gone.

****

Commodore Blanton had returned to the *Rom* and was just settling back into his command when Glenn, the sonar tech, started waving at him frantically.

"Commodore!" Glenn called.

Blanton moved to stand behind Glenn at his station.

"The Kraken is back. It's approaching the combined forces of DESRON 49 and DESRON 13 from the north. It's coming in slower this time. I don't know why."

Blanton studied the screen in front of Glenn. "Where are the megalodons?"

"They've withdrawn to a position behind our ships," Glenn explained.

"All of them?" Blanton demanded.

"All of them, sir," Glenn confirmed. "At least the eighteen that are still alive."

Blanton ground his teeth together. Inwardly, he cursed Dr. Hydely for his unauthorized attack on the Kraken with a portion of the megalodon strength that was now also under his command. That attack had cost the lives of six of the sharks. It also left Dr. Hydely in a state where his ability to control the others was questionable at best. Still, Blanton would have expected more from Hydely's genetically engineered killing machines than them retreating behind the ships of the two DESRONs.

"Something is happening with the Kraken, sir," Glenn told him.

The image representing the Kraken on the sonar screen suddenly resembled that of a sub launching volley after volley of torpedoes. Hundreds of smaller dots came into existence on the screen, streaking away from the Kraken, on a direct route for the ships on Blanton's command.

"Sound battle stations!" Blanton shouted. "What the devil are those things, Glenn?"

"I don't know, sir, but they're coming in fast."

****

The *Stanz*'s position in the intermixed formation of DESRON 49 and DESRON 13 put it closest to the approaching Kraken. The Kraken, though, had launched something, or rather a lot of somethings, at the DESRONs and then veered away from them on a new course.

Petty Officer Rita Mullens stood on the port side of the *Stanz*, accompanied by a heavily armed response team. She stared at the water through her pair of binoculars, not quite sure what to expect from the approaching waves of contacts. The ship's C.I.W.S. had already opened fire. With a continuous roar of booming thunder, it spat a stream of high-velocity rounds at whatever was coming their way.

Mullens could make out black patches in the water. She knew the Kraken's blood was black, but the Kraken had veered away from the ships, and the patches of black were spread out over a great distance.

It wasn't until the first of the squids reached the *Stanz* and started climbing up at the side of its hull that she knew what she was facing. Dozens and dozens of smaller squid-like creatures attached themselves to the *Stanz*, using their primary two tentacles to scale up its side with unbelievable speed.

"Don't let them board!" she heard the lead officer of the response team order in the moment before he and his personnel opened fire on the squids. Small arms fire erupted all around Mullens. She dropped her binoculars, trying to cover her ears. She wasn't trained for this kind of up-close combat. Mullens wanted to run, but there was nowhere to run to. The response team was all about her, blazing away, downward, over the side of the ship.

Several squids took rounds that blew them apart. Others lost tentacles to the rain of ammo that hammered onto them but kept on coming. She saw the right primary tentacle of one squid go flying from its body in a spray of black blood. It dangled from the side of the ship, held in place by its left tentacle's club, which remained buried in the metal of the ship's hull. It swung there helplessly until a shotgun blast from another member of the response team pulped its main body, leaving nothing more than a black smear on the side of the *Stanz*.

The squids were coming over the side railing now. They sprang into the ranks of the response team. Tentacles whipped about, tearing flesh. Other squids used their primary tentacles like spears, stabbing at the men and women trying to hold them back.

The response team's CO gave a pained grunt where he stood next to her as something wet and warm splashed over Mullens. She turned to see the man had been impaled by a tentacle. It had been thrust completely through his chest, and its tip was whipping about in the air behind the man where it had emerged through his back. The man's blood was all over her.

Mullens screamed then. She shoved past a soldier who was trying to get a shot at squid that was busy gnawing away at the throat of a woman. It had its tentacles wrapped around where the two of them lay on the deck. The man cursed, his shot going wild, but Mullens made it by him.

She didn't look back. Her only thought was to get back inside the ship. Her legs pumped under her as her breath came in ragged gasps. Mullens didn't see the squid that hurled itself over the side of the ship at her until it struck her. The thing's lower tentacles ensnared her waist as one of its main two tentacles curled around her throat. The barbs that ran the length of each tentacle's underside dug into her, drawing blood, but it was the one about her throat that ended her life. It squeezed there with such force, Mullens' head was severed from her body. It bounced onto the deck and rolled off the ship to splash into the ocean water below.

****

"Reports are coming in from all over the new combined task force, sir!" Allen told Blanton. "We're under attack!"

"By what?" Blanton frowned. "The Kraken veered away from our position!"

"It appears the Kraken deployed hundreds of smaller, mutated squids. They're unlike anything anyone has ever seen before. They are scaling the hull's of the taskforce's ships and boarding them."

"God have mercy on us," Blanton said aloud. "This nightmare just keeps getting worse and worse."

"The automatic fire of the ships' C.I.W.S. and the quick thinking of some of our captains who fired at the approaching contacts seem to have greatly reduced the number of lesser squids before they really hit us, or we would be in a lot worse shape."

"How bad is it?" Blanton asked.

"We've lost contact with both frigates, and the *Stanz* is under heavy attack. She's been boarded, sir. Her response teams and onboard marines are doing their best but..."

"But the *Stanz* is barely hanging on," Blanton finished for her.

Allen gave him a grim nod.

"Get on the comm and order all ships in the task force to seal up. If those things make it aboard any more of them, that action might keep the fighting contained to their exterior decks."

"Yes, sir!" Allen snapped. "Good thinking, sir!"

Blanton whirled on his weapons officer. "If you get a shot at any of those things out there, take it."

"They are very fast and small targets, sir, but I will do my best!"

"See that you do," Blanton snarled.

"Allen!" Blanton called.

She came rushing back to his side.

"Are we clear of the things?"

"Yes, sir," Allen assured him. "The *Rom* hasn't been targeted by those things yet, at least not more so than our C.I.W.S. can handle. Our decks are clear."

Blanton relaxed some, though not much, from that news.

"The megalodons are moving, sir!" Glenn nearly leaped from his chair with excitement. "They're swinging around the task force to engage the lesser squids!"

"Who is controlling them?" Allen asked, and by the look of her, she was feeling the same level of shock that Glenn was.

Blanton's communications officer spoke up. "Captain Flecker says the megalodons are acting on their own, sir."

A smile crept onto Blanton's lips. "Go get 'em," he laughed, cheering the sharks on.

The shark's move came too late to save the *Stanz* and the taskforce's two frigates. Those ships were overrun and lost. However, the megalodons made short work of the lesser squids still in the water. Eighteen weaponized behemoths swept into the ranks of the lesser squids, shattering them. The lesser squids were no match for the megalodons. The battle was over in mere minutes with only one megalodon lost. Perhaps that one shark had shown too much bravado or perhaps it was just unlucky. Either way, its path had taken into the very center of the lesser squids. They had swarmed it. Dozens and dozens of them latching onto its massive body and tearing at its flesh like a school of piranha. The megalodon's ripped and shredded corpse sunk into the depths as the other megalodons came for their vengeance, making short work of the squids that had killed their brother.

"That was the last of them, sir," Glenn told Blanton. "The water is clear, and there is no sign of the Kraken."

Though not knowing where the Mother Kraken worried Blanton, he happily called the battle a victory. Things could have been a lot worse had the megalodons not opted to intervene on their own. As it was, the destruction of the *Stanz* along with the taskforce's two frigates stung badly enough. The loss of their guns would be keenly felt when the Kraken next returned. The *Stanz* had blown herself. Blanton didn't really know why. He knew the squids swarming the ship had penetrated even her most interior decks and her bridge. The final communication Blanton had received from the ship before it blossomed into an orange ball of flame and flying shrapnel hadn't been from her captain, but a petty officer, who claimed to be the ship's acting CO as all of the ranking officers were dead or missing.

The frigates with their smaller crews and lesser amount of weapons were adrift on the waves. When Blanton had taken a look at them through a pair of binoculars brought to him by one of his aides, he had seen the lesser squids still on those ships. They were all over their sides and exterior decks like swarming ants. Had the rest of the taskforce's situation not been so dire with the Mother Kraken still out there, he would have tried to take them back by force. That wasn't an option for the time being, though. He needed all his resources at hand to deal with the Mother Kraken. The two frigates simply had to be written off and their loss accepted.

Blanton had a quick chat with Dr. Hydely, who was nearly recovered and almost ready to be released from medical. The doctor had confirmed Blanton's suspicions that the lesser squids were indeed likely the Kraken's offspring. That was why he now referred to the great beast that was stalking his task force as the Mother Kraken and not just Kraken anymore.

Dr. Hydely was excited by what the Kraken's use of its young as cannon fodder seemed to imply. He speculated that the Kraken had either been pregnant at the time it entered its long slumber on the ocean floor or reproduced at an utterly astonishing rate that defied modern scientific explanation. Hydely leaned towards the latter being the case. As wondrous as Dr. Hydely might find the Mother Kraken's ability to reproduce, if he was correct, it created an entirely new problem for Blanton and his task force. Blanton was forced to admit that his plan had been to escape the Kraken, not destroy it. If the creature reproduced so quickly, however, it was his duty to stop it here and now. Left unchecked, the Mother Kraken could produce enough offspring in a matter of weeks to have an entire army at its command. That simply could not be allowed to happen.

"Allen," Blanton called at his XO. "Get Dr. Hydely and Nicholson to my ready room ASAP and set up a meeting with the other captains over comms. We need some kind of plan before that monster comes at us again."

****

Blanton, Dr. Hydely, and Nicholson sat in Blanton's ready room. All the surviving captains of the newly merged task force were present as well via comms link.

Blanton got the meeting rolling. "Dr. Hydely, I know you want to control the sharks for our coming battle with the Kraken, but I am assigning that duty to Captain Flecker."

Dr. Hydely went berserk with rage to the point that Lieutenant Nicholson had to physically restrain the doctor to keep the man from hurling himself at Blanton, intent on tearing the commodore apart by tooth and nail.

Captain Flecker protested as well. "Commodore Blanton, are you sure this is a wise move to make? The doctor has much more experience with the sharks than I do."

"I am aware of that, Captain Flecker, but Dr. Hydely isn't military. As brilliant as he may be, the good doctor lacks your combat experience and *feel* for tactical situations."

"You can't do this!" Dr. Hydely cried, struggling against Nicholson's hold on him. "Those are my sharks! They're my life's work!"

"I am sorry, Doctor, but the call is mine and I have made it. There will be no more discussion of this," Blanton said firmly, ignoring Hydely as he continued to rage against the decision.

"Lieutenant Nicholson, if you would kindly remove Dr. Hydely from the room so that this meeting can continue."

Moments later, after Dr. Hydely had been escorted out, Blanton continued. "I want every ship in the task force to be sealed up tight before we engage the Kraken again. All exterior doors that aren't essential need to be welded shut if possible. Those that this can't be done to, need to have ready response teams assigned to them. We all saw what happened to the *Stanz* and those two frigates. If the Kraken deploys more of those lesser squids, we need to be ready for them."

"Yes, sir," chorused the voices of the captains over their comms.

"Good," Blanton nodded. "Now, we also need a means of taking out the Kraken herself. That has to be our priority. As much as I would like us to be able to just run from that monster and return with more ships, we can't. At the rate it may be reproducing, according to Dr. Hydely, we need to destroy that thing here and now. Any suggestions?"

"I thought the megalodons were our plan for dealing with the Kraken?" Flecker reminded him.

"They are," Blanton said, "but we can't count on them to get the job done. If something goes wrong and we lose control of them or they aren't up to the task, we need a backup plan."

"I know how to kill that monster for sure." The image of Captain Peek showed off the grin she wore on her lips. "But you're not going to like it, sir."

"Let me guess." Blanton smirked. "Use one our ships as bait, lure the Kraken to it, and then blow it sky high while the Kraken has it in its grip?"

Peek's grin became an expression of shock. "How did you know, sir?"

"Lieutenant Nicholson suggested the same course of action earlier. I wasn't ready to admit we were that desperate then but now…"

"If we have to kill it and make sure it's dead, assuming the megalodons fail, I agree that something like that is our best bet," Flecker said, nodding.

"The question then becomes which ship do we sacrifice?" Shelby, the newly acting CO of the *Harrell*, chimed in. The ship's captain had suffered an unexpected heart attack that left Shelby, as its XO, to step up and assume command.

"It can't be the *Leary*." Flecker smiled, knowing his ship couldn't afford to be lost until the megalodons were all out for the count. "It's the only ship in this task force with the gear to control the sharks."

"It can't be the *Rom* either," Captain Peek said. "The *Rom* is not only our flagship, but she has the best comms gear of any ship here. And frankly, sir," Peek's gaze focused on Blanton, "we can't afford to lose you either. Yes, we have lost a lot of ships between our two DESRONs, but without your quick thinking so far, we might have lost all of them to that monster already."

Blanton felt his cheeks flush slightly at Peek's unexpected praise. Clearing his throat, he said, "Thank you for that, Captain Peek. Not sure I deserve such praise given where we stand."

Hesitantly, Acting Captain Shelby surprised everyone by offering the *Harrell* as the bait to lure in the Kraken. When the others had recovered from their surprise, she continued, "It just makes sense. I am the lowest ranking officer, and the *Harrell* isn't as important to this mission as the *Rom* or the *Leary*."

"You're sure you want to do this?" Blanton questioned her.

"Yes, Commodore, I do." Shelby nodded again.

"So be it." Blanton popped the joints of the fingers on his right hand. "The *Harrell* will be our bait. I want all nonessential personnel transferred off her to other ships as quickly as possible. As that is being done, we'll load her down with enough explosives in addition to her own stockpiles to be sure that when the Kraken takes her, she will be the last ship that thing ever wraps its tentacles around."

"I guess we're done here then," Flecker commented.

"You're all dismissed," Blanton told the others. "We've got a lot of work to do before that thing comes back so we best get started on it."

****

XO Laura Shelby was nervous as she took the command chair on the *Harrell*'s bridge. She had always dreamed of her own command, but she had never wanted it like this. She had respected and liked the ship's captain a great deal. The sudden heart attack the captain had suffered had come at the worst possible time, leaving her stuck with the crew depending on her and her first real command being a literal trial by fire.

Shelby had been in the Navy for over six years now and worked her way up to XO very quickly thanks to her astounding organizational skills and her habit of not taking crap from anyone. She thought of herself as a very capable officer, but she also knew she wasn't ready for this. That was one of the reasons she had offered the *Harrell* up as bait for the Kraken. She didn't want to die. No one in their right mind did, but sometimes you had to do what was best for the greater good. Shelby knew her parents would have been proud of the call she had made in doing so.

She watched the stream of small boats leaving the ship, packed full with men and women lucky enough to be escaping its fate. The only personnel staying aboard were herself, the bridge crew, a group of engineers and damage control folks, and the ship's ready response teams.

Shelby supposed she could hope that Flecker and Dr. Hydely's megalodons would stop the Kraken, but she felt it was better not to carry that hope. Those of her crew staying aboard with her deserved more than that. It was better they accepted death now and be ready for it if it came.

"You okay, ma'am?" Gannon, her weapons officer, asked.

"Just thinking I guess." Shelby shrugged.

"Well, don't you worry about the weapon systems, ma'am," Gannon assured her. "If that monster gets by the sharks, everything we got is primed and ready to go."

Shelby feigned comfort at hearing Gannon's words. She knew those weapons he was so proud of wouldn't be enough, and she suspected that deep down Gannon knew it too.

****

There were still several hours of daylight left when the Kraken showed itself again. It came sweeping in towards the taskforce from the north. Blanton ordered all the ships to change course to engage it. This time, he was taking the offensive, and Flecker was glad that he was.

Flecker missed being on the *Leary*'s bridge. He knew that Robbins could handle the ship, but he would have much rather been there himself than in Hydely's lab. With a sigh, he slipped the control helmet the doctor had designed on and plugged it in. The interface with the megalodons was instant and slammed into his mind like the balled-up fist of a brawler's hand. His body was jarred by the mental impact.

Flecker blinked as the room around him vanished to be replaced by the senses of the megalodons he was now a part of. He felt the ocean water on him. It was cool and helped him focus so he could sort through the various streams, determining which shark each belonged to and their position in the water in relation to the approaching Kraken. Each of the sharks was distinct and different. Their thoughts and attitudes poured into him. Curry's had by far the greatest impression on him. Curry was the group's alpha, the largest and smartest of Dr. Hydely's creations. Most of the sharks felt some trace of fear at the sight of the Kraken. It was as if some primordial part of their minds told them it was the apex predator of the waters it traveled through and they needed to steer clear of it. That fear was only a trace, though. Each of the sharks, especially Curry, was designed by Hydely to overcome such things and turn those types of feelings into aggression. Flecker felt that aggression growing inside them, their fear turning to a hunger for the Kraken's flesh.

The sharks raced through the water to meet the approaching monster as it grew closer to the task force. They were its first line of attack, and Flecker hoped they would live up to Dr. Hydely's expectations of them.

Flecker sensed what Curry wanted to do. The alpha megalodon wanted to use the sharks' numbers to close on the Kraken and overwhelm it. Flecker figured that was as good a plan as any, and it certainly had its charms. He let Curry take control of the overall group, though he kept himself ready to jump in mentally and override any Curry's tactical choices if things hit the fan.

The Kraken had faced the sharks, though in lesser numbers, once before and appeared ready for them this time. It retracted its tentacles for close-in defense as the sharks came at it in wide-spread groups. Each group dove at the Kraken from a different vector, putting their numbers to use. The giant squid allowed them to draw close before it lashed out at them. Its two primary tentacles stabbed outwards. Each of them pierced a megalodon, stabbing into and through the bodies of two sharks, as the tips of the tentacles exited the sharks' bodies from the opposite side that they had entered. Entrails and blood burst outward with the exiting tips of the tentacles, turning the water around the two sharks into clouds of red.

Its other tentacles took a less direct approach, though a no less deadly one. They grabbed at the sharks as they approached. Each of the Kraken's six lesser tentacles ensnared a megalodon and held it in a death grip. The megalodons were designed to take a good deal of damage, their skeletal structures superior and denser than that of any other living creature's in the oceans except for perhaps the Kraken they now fought. Even so, the six tentacles squeezed with such powerful pressure that the caught megalodons trashed about in their grasp as they were crushed like eggs.

The Kraken, as fast as it was, didn't have the time for another attack before Curry and the other megalodons reached it. They charged in, taking large bites from the Kraken's central mass that left the giant squid leaking gallons of its black, oil-like blood into the water as they sped away.

The monster whirled on them, trying to get in another full-out attack before the megalodons were out of its reach. Only its two main tentacles were long enough to get in blows on the retreating sharks. The club-like hooked tip of its right tentacle caught one of the megalodons in its back, embedding itself there. Its tip cut the shark apart like the blade of a knife as the megalodon continued to try to flee, and the Kraken pulled its tentacle back simultaneously. The entire rear half of the megalodon's body was cut in two. As soon as the tip of the tentacles had cut its way free, the body of the already-dead megalodon spun away in the water, rolling over and over as it angled downwards towards the ocean floor. The Kraken's other main tentacle hit a megalodon like a whip, wrapping around it. The strength of the tentacle jerked the giant shark to a sudden halt. Flecker felt every second of the shark's fear as it struggled to break free. Thankfully for Flecker, that struggle was a short one. He could feel the bards of the tentacle's underside slashing away at the skin of the captured megalodon in the moments before the tentacle contracted and ended the giant shark's life.

The feedback from the death of the sharks was almost too much for Flecker. He handled better than Dr. Hydely had, but it took all his will to do so. Flecker managed to stay interfaced with the megalodons, but continued to allow Curry to lead the sharks' attack on the Kraken.

The remaining megalodons followed Curry as they swung around to make another run at the Kraken. Over half their number had been lost in the first attack. Flecker could sense that if it were not for Curry, the others might have broken off the engagement with the Kraken altogether despite their programming.

Just as the Kraken had learned from its first encounter with the megalodons, the sharks had learned as well. This time, as the Kraken's tentacles snaked outward to meet them, three megalodons went after them. Two of the megalodons were successful. Their massive teeth sunk into the flesh of the tentacles that came for them. They bit deep. One of them thrashed about in the water as it wrestled with the tentacle it held in its mouth. The other successful megalodon actually managed to bite one of the Kraken's lesser tentacles to the point that it was severed. The upper third of it drifted away from the Kraken as the megalodon sped away, its wounded end spurting bursts of black blood.

Of the three who went for the tentacles and failed, one was almost successful but not quite. It managed to bit into the tentacle it had gone after, wounding the limb, but the tentacle had coiled around its body in the process. Barbs tore at its skin as a red cloud of blood formed around where it struggled against the tentacle's hold. In the end, it was able to bite the tentacle in two but paid the ultimate price for its victory. The length of tentacle still wrapped around it shredded its skin from its body as the shark broke free, only to bleed out moments later and drift upwards towards the ocean's surface.

The other two megalodons simply weren't fast enough. The Kraken's tentacles whipped them away, bashing in the head of one of the megalodons in the process. The other was struck on its underside as the tentacle sliced along the length of its body. Though dead, with its intestines protruding from its open belly, the megalodon swam on, carried along by its momentum.

The attack on its tentacles had thrown the order of the Kraken's planned defense into chaos. Its other tentacles missed all of the other sharks with Curry that closed on it except one.

That one died as one of the Kraken's primary tentacles speared it and shook its body about in anger and frustration.

Curry and the three megalodons with him reached the Kraken's main body. One of the sharks caught a tentacle at its base. Its razor teeth closed around the tentacle, severing it from the Kraken's body in an explosion of black oil-like blood. The Kraken, for once, reeled in pain. Its body shifted even as the rest of the megalodons plowed into it. Curry rammed it, hard, caving in a section of the central body, before managing to get in a bite that drew blood before he twisted away from the Kraken and fled its counter attack. The other two megalodons with him got in their own bites as well, razor teeth rending Kraken flesh and tearing chunks from its main body. Then all the surviving megalodons were once again following Curry to build up speed and swing about for another attack.

This time, the Kraken followed them. It threw itself after the sharks, going after them in a berserker-like fury. Though it was missing a tentacle and another was dragged along in the water, leaking black blood, its two primary ones strived to inflict vengeance upon the megalodons. Both tentacles targeted Curry. It was as if the Kraken sensed that Curry was the megalodons' alpha. Curry rolled in the water, dodging the first. It cut through the water where the giant shark had been a mere second before. Curry zagged in an attempt to elude the second, but his luck had run out. The tentacle's hook-like club caught Curry in his side. Curry's speed allowed the giant shark to rip free of it but not without the tentacle accomplishing its goal of taking Curry out of the fight.

The wound it inflicted on Curry was a lethal one. It had sliced him all along his right side, deep into his body. The explosion of red that burst from Curry blossomed outward into a cloud to the point that Flecker lost sight of Curry through the eyes of the other megalodons. He knew Curry was dead, though. He had felt the giant shark die and heard Curry's final mental cries of pain and fear within his own mind.

That did prove too much for Flecker. The synaptic pathways of his mind blazed as they overloaded. Flecker screamed a final scream and then was nothing more than an empty sack of flesh sitting in the lab's control chair.

With both Flecker and Curry gone, the remaining megalodons gave up their fight. They fled the scene of the battle, doing their best to escape the raging Kraken that continued to pursue them.

****

"Is he dead?" Nicholson asked, staring at Flecker. Blood leaked from the corners of Flecker's eyes and rivers of red ran from his ears and nose.

"In a sense," Dr. Hydely told him. "Flecker experienced a synaptic overload that cooked his brain inside his skull. His body is still alive, but there's nothing left of who he was."

Nicholson made the sign of the cross over his chest before he moved to reach out and close Flecker's eyes. He couldn't take the emptiness of them. Seeing people getting shot or being blown apart, those were things that Nicholson was used to. The kind of death Flecker had just died unsettled him at his core.

Dr. Hydely went on about his work, utterly unconcerned with what had happened to Flecker. Tears slid from the doctor's eyes to flow over his cheeks, but Nicholson knew they were for the megalodons that were lost in the battle.

"I'm sorry about your sharks," Nicholson offered, placing a hand on Hydely's shoulder in an attempt to comfort the doctor.

Hydely shook it away. "Don't be sorry, Lieutenant. We learned a lot here today."

"I can see you're hurting, Doc," Nicholson told him.

"Nonsense," Hydely lied. "Not all of my megalodons were lost. You'll see to it that Commodore Blanton helps me round them up after this mess with the Kraken is over with, won't you?"

"Sure, Doc." Nicholson frowned, wondering if Hydely even realized that the odds weren't in favor of any of them being still alive when the Kraken was done. The megalodons had been the task force's best hope of stopping the Kraken and they had failed. The megalodons had done a good deal of damage to the Kraken, yes, but the beast was very much still alive and royally ticked off.

The doctor's disregard for the loss of Flecker wore on Nicholson, but there was nothing he could do about it. Hydely was who he was and getting on his case about it wouldn't change anything. It would only create strife between the two of them.

And since it was his job to make sure the doctor was both safe and kept out of the commodore's way, Nicholson did his best to keep his mouth shut.

Nicholson moved to the comms unit on the lab's wall and radioed the bridge.

"Nicholson here," he said. "The megalodons have failed. I repeat, the megalodons have failed to stop the Kraken."

"Lieutenant Nicholson?" Robbins voiced answered. "Where's Captain Flecker?"

"Flecker is dead, sir," Nicholson reported. "The feedback from the megalodons lost in the battle was too much for him."

There was a pause before Robbins responded. "Understood."

Nicholson had done what was required of him. He turned back to Hydely who was busy continuing to try to track the remaining megalodons as they fled the Kraken.

"Look, Doc, we need to get Flecker's body to medical so they can deal with it," he said.

"You do that if you must, Lieutenant," Hydely said, barely paying him any attention. "I have much work to do here. Monitoring the megalodons now will save us a great deal of time when we go looking for them later."

Nicholson gritted his teeth. He couldn't leave the doctor alone. Stripping off his jacket, he used it to cover Flecker's body as best he could. He really wanted to grab Hydely and beat some sense into the man.

****

Commodore Blanton slammed a fist into the arm of his command chair when he heard the news that the megalodons had failed. Glenn confirmed it via the sonar. The remaining sharks were high-tailing it away from the approaching Kraken. The Kraken's speed had slowed. It was clearly wounded, but yet it continued on towards the task force.

Blanton gestured for his comms officer to patch him into the captains who were awaiting his orders. "All ships, target the Kraken. I want the monster dead before it gets any closer to us."

One of the ships of the task force opened fire. Missiles flew from their launchers to streak through the air before descending upon their target. Waves of water flew skyward as the dived into the depths and detonated, but the Kraken still came on. Volley after volley of torpedoes left their tubes. They met the Kraken a good distance out from the ships of the task force. Explosions raged beneath the waves. One volley struck and then the next and the next.

Commodore Blanton got up from his command chair and moved to peer out the *Rom*'s forward window. He could tell exactly where the Kraken was because it was leaving a stream of black blood in its wake. It was closing on the task force fast.

"Tell Acting Captain Shelby that she's up," Blanton ordered. Even as he gave the command, he watched the USS *Harrell* maneuvering to engage the Kraken. He said a silent prayer for Shelby and those aboard the *Harrell* with her. None of them deserved to die. Most of those onboard the *Harrell* had families.

Many of them were young, too, with a lot of life left ahead of them. They were going to pay the ultimate price, though, so the rest of the taskforce could live.

"Get me a channel to the *Harrell*," Blanton ordered. "And keep it open."

"Yes, sir," his comms officer shouted back.

"Acting Captain Shelby, what is your status?" Blanton asked.

"We are moving to intercept the Kraken now, sir," Shelby answered. Her voice was thick with emotion. Blanton could almost feel her fear despite the distance between them as if it was a tangible force.

Blanton rubbed at his stubble-covered cheeks. He wondered if the stress and exhaustion were getting to him because he almost wished he was with Shelby on the *Harrell*'s bridge.

"Commodore," Shelby said, "the Kraken appears to be taking the bait. My sonar tech has lost it on his screen, but believes the Kraken has slowed and dived in the water, likely to come up below us as it did with the *Bunn*."

Blanton didn't know how to respond. What did one say to a captain who they had just ordered to their death?

He heard Shelby screaming orders over the comms before the transmission went dead.

"We've lost contact with the *Harrell*, sir!" his comms officer shouted.

Blanton could see why. The Kraken had come up from below the *Harrell* just as Shelby had guessed it would. Long tentacles emerged from the water as they wrapped themselves around the destroyer's hull. Several of them were slicked black with the creature's own blood. The end of one of the tentacles was badly mangled, but that didn't stop the rest of its length from curling around the aft section of the *Harrell.*

"Get me Shelby back!" Blanton snapped.

"I can't, sir," the comms officer told him, on the edge of panic.

"Get it together, sir," Allen said, suddenly moving to get into his face.

Blanton nearly took a swing at her before he caught himself. Allen looked just as ticked off as he felt.

"We knew this was going to happen, sir," she said. "This was the plan. You approved it."

Blanton knew she was right. Everything she said made perfect sense. He had approved the plan. He had sentenced all those poor sailors to their death. He felt the weight of that call bearing down on him now. It took him a moment, but he managed to regain his composure.

"Sorry, Allen," he said sincerely and took a step back from where she stood. "Just give me some space, okay?"

Allen nodded. "This is the right call, sir," she assured him. "Besides, it's too late to change anyway."

Blanton stared out the window at the Kraken and the *Harrell.* He could see the metal of the ship's hull beginning to give under the pressure the monster was applying on it. Shelby didn't have long to make her move. The explosives the *Harrell* carried on her had to be activated. Part of him wondered why Shelby hadn't set them off already. Maybe she was clinging to every second of life she had left. He didn't know and never would.

Without warning, the *Harrell* became a flash of light and fire. Flames leaped up towards the sky as pieces of the destroyer's shattering hull spun outward and away from the center of the blast.

"Brace for impact!" Allen yelled.

Blanton grabbed a hold of the edge of the nearest console and steadied himself. The size of the blast from the *Harrell* was to going to create some mega shockwaves. The waves came rolling into the rest of the taskforce. The *Rom* and the other ships shook, tossed about the ocean's surface as the shockwaves hammered into them. Their impact caused Blanton to ram his right knee into the console he was holding on to. He gave a grunt of pain and saw a patch of red forming on his pants above the wound he had just taken. Blanton dropped to his left knee, grimacing. Still, he considered himself lucky as he looked about the *Rom*'s bridge.

Allen had been flung into the forward window. Her crumpled body lay below, unmoving, and her blood streaked its glass. She had hit it with enough force to cause hairline cracks in its reinforced surface. Blanton figured she was dead until he realized she was moaning. Her moans were hard to hear through the chaos surrounding them. Several consoles had shorted out around the bridge, spraying showers of sparks before bursting into flames.

Blanton breathed a sigh of relief as he saw a damage control team accompanied by a pair of medics come racing through the bridge's entrance. The damage control team hosed the raging fires with extinguishers and helped the lesser wounded to their feet.

"Over here!" Blanton cried. One of the medics came rushing up to him.

"How badly are you hurt, sir?" the medic asked with wide eyes.

"Not me," Blanton raged at the woman. "Her!"

He pointed at Allen. He saw the medic's expression as she glanced at Allen and could tell his guess at Allen being dead hadn't been too far off.

"Stay here, sir," the medic ordered him. "I'll do what I can for her."

To Hell with that, Blanton thought. He had a ship to run, and his first priority was making sure that monster out there was dead. Blanton used the console next to him to pull himself up. His right leg refused to work correctly. He looked down at it and saw a shard of white bone protruding from the center of the red that stained the pants covering his lower leg. Blanton nearly threw up right then and there but somehow managed to hold it together. Fighting the pain, he hobbled through the mess the

Rom's bridge had become to his command chair and half-sat, half-fell into it.

"Status!" he barked at no one in particular.

Glenn's voice answered him. "Damage reports coming in from all over, sir! Those shockwaves nearly tore the ship apart. We're taking on water in some of the forward sections, but it's nothing our pumps and damage teams can't handle."

The sonar station was one of the few still functioning areas of the bridge, and Glenn's worst injury looked to be a growing bruise on that stretched over the backside of his left hand.

"Casualties?"

"Fifteen confirmed dead so far, sir." Glenn frowned. "Five times that injured reported already."

"And the task force?"

"All ships accounted for, Commodore Blanton." Glenn smiled, but his expression quickly changed as he spoke again, "Except for the *Harrell* of course, sir. She's gone."

Blanton had been examining his own wounded leg as Glenn talked. In the process, one of his fingertips accidently rubbed the bone sticking out of his leg. The contact sent fire blazing throughout Blanton's body. He had to close his eyes, tilting his head back, until the pain passed. When he was able to think again, he started to ask about the Kraken, but realized Glenn was already telling him.

"I have the Kraken on my screen, sir. From how it's moving, the Kraken appears to be badly hurt but very much still alive."

It took Blanton a moment to realize that Glenn had just told him that thing out there was still alive. It didn't have any right in Hell to be, but it was.

"Frag it," Blanton swore, shoving a medic who had knelt in front of him to treat his leg away.

"Not now!" he roared at the startled medic at his feet then turned his attention back to Glenn. "What's it doing?"

"Nothing, sir," Glenn told him. "It might be in shock or stunned. It seems to be drifting in the water and barely maintaining its position just below the surface of the waves."

Blanton started to order his comms officer to open a channel to the other ships but noticed that the officer was dead and sprawled out on the deck. Burns covered still-smoking arms, and the officer's face was a mass of mangled meat from the comms station that had exploded.

"Can you patch me through to the rest of the taskforce?" Blanton asked.

Glenn nodded excitedly. "I've been rerouting controls for all the systems that I can to my station sir. I should be able to."

"Do it!" Blanton snapped.

Glenn gestured to him that it had been done.

"All ships still able to do so, target the Kraken and hit that bastard with everything you have got!"

The *Leary* came about in the water. Its bow turned to face the drifting form of the Kraken. Her forward tubes spat torpedoes. First two, followed by two more, before a third and final volley emptied her launchers. The first volley struck the Kraken. The waters churned as they detonated, black oil-like blood splashing upwards. The second volley and third volley blew entire sections of the Kraken's body apart. As they did so, the giant monster seemed to come awake. Its body shook in spasms beneath the waves, tentacles twitching as if finding new life.

The *Peterson* was closer to the monster than either the *Leary* or the *Rom*. It was so close to the Kraken in range that its C.I.W.S. thundered on its deck. High-velocity rounds stabbed at the bleeding monster, biting into its main body. The Kraken surged forward in fury, targeting the *Peterson*. It poured on speed as it closed on the ship at an impossible rate.

"The Kraken is moving again, Commodore Blanton!" Glenn shouted. "It's going after the *Peterson*!"

Blanton had allowed the medic he had shoved away to bandage and brace his leg. He threw himself from his command chair, ignoring the pain that tried to overwhelm him, to hobble to Glenn's side at the sonar station. He stared at the sonar screen over Glenn's shoulder.

"By all that's holy, no!" Blanton gasped. He wanted to scream to the ship's captain to get out of the monster's path but knew his words would come too late to make any difference for Peek and her crew.

The Kraken rammed the *Peterson* at a speed of forty knots. The destroyer tilted on the waves from the force of the impact, nearly rolling over. It was lifted from the water as its hull split apart along its port side. Something inside the *Peterson* exploded. Whatever it was, it set off a chain reaction of secondary explosions that raged all over the destroyer. Then in a flash, the *Peterson* was gone, just like the *Harrell*.

"Where is the Kraken?" Blanton yelled at Glenn so close he saw the sonar tech wince from the pain he had just inflicted on his eardrums.

"I don't know, sir!" Glenn shouted back, his fingers dancing over the controls of the sonar station.

"Find it!" Blanton ordered. "We need to know where that thing is, now!"

"I believe it was destroyed by the explosions that took out the *Peterson*, sir," Glenn told him.

"Confirm that," Blanton growled.

"Doing my best, sir," Glenn answered, working hard to do just that.

Seconds ticked by like hours as Blanton waited for Glenn to do his job.

"I've got confirmation, sir," another sailor shouted from where he stood near the bridge's main window.

"Help me," Blanton demanded of Glenn. Glenn got up, leaving his station, to support Blanton as the two of them headed across the bridge.

The sailor who had shouted at them was pointing out through the window. Blanton looked out and took a startled breath as he saw what the sailor was pointing at. Chunks of the Kraken were floating on the surface of the ocean amid the debris from the *Peterson*.

"Thank God," Blanton muttered, running a hand through his sweat-slicked hair. "It's finally over."

****

Four hours later, after having his leg properly treated and a solid two hours of sleep, Commodore Blanton had returned to the *Rom*'s bridge. He had checked in on Allen during that time as well. Medical was overrun with wounded, and the staff there was pushed to their limits. Even given her rank, his XO, had been hard to find amid the dozens upon dozens of wounded and dead who spilled out of medical into the corridor beyond its entrance. He had asked two of the doctors and a nurse where Allen was before he finally located her. She had died from her impact with the bridge window, most of her bones shattered. The doctors said it was the internal bleeding that got her, though. Her corpse had been bagged and left to be processed along with the other dead at the edge of the makeshift triage area the doctors had set up. Blanton had unzipped the bag to confirm it was her himself. The beauty she had in life was gone, and all was that remained was a body so broken and swollen he barely recognized her. Her death had hit him hard. On some levels, harder than anything that he had just lived through. He had always hoped that somehow, maybe one day he would prove to her he wasn't the screw up she acted like he was and the two of them would hook up. Now, that was impossible. The Kraken had taken her from him.

As he eased himself into his command chair, he took stock of the state of the repairs going on around the bridge. Things were already looking much better. Helm control had been restored, and engineering was reporting that all the water had been pumped out of the damaged areas of the ship where its hull had been ruptured.

He had promoted Glenn and made the sonar tech his new XO. Glenn had taken the job like a fish to water, and given how the repairs were coming, Blanton could see he had made the right choice.

Petty Officer Lancaster had taken over the sonar station in Glenn's absence. Lancaster had the training, though she lacked Glenn's experience at the job.

Blanton checked in with Robbins aboard the *Leary* and was glad to hear that Robbins ship was in an even better state than the *Rom*. Robbins was holding surprisingly well himself. Blanton knew that Robbins and Flecker had been close. He imagined that Flecker's death had hit Robbins as hard as the loss of Allen had struck him.

It was nearly impossible to believe that the Kraken had done so much damage and stopping the monster had cost so many lives. The *Rom* and the *Leary* were all that remained of the task force that once had been composed of two DESRON, now merely two ships.

After hearing that Robbins and his ship were ready to move, Blanton gave the order for the two destroyers left under his command to set a new course. It took a few more minutes to plot their course and get underway but at last, they were headed home.

****

Acting Captain Robbins paced the bridge of the *Leary*. It felt strange being in command. He missed Flecker greatly. The crew missed Flecker as well. Robbins' knew his style of command was much more gruff and by the book than Flecker's had ever been. He was sure the crew was thankful that they only had to endure him a few more days until they reached a safe harbor.

Compared to the *Rom*, the *Leary* had taken very little damage. She hadn't been as close to the *Harrell* when Acting Captain Shelby had blown it in an attempt to destroy the Kraken. She had failed to do it, but none the less wounded the beast so greatly that the remainder of the task force had been able to finish it.

Dr. Hydely continued to hassle him about rounding up the surviving megalodons. The doctor didn't appear to understand the word "no." Hydely has also requested numerous times for Robbins to turn the ship about in order to collect a piece of the dead Kraken so that Hydely could study the creature's DNA. The doctor believed it was vital to learn as much as possible about the Kraken. Robbins didn't see it that way. He was content to let the Kraken's corpse be disposed of by nature. What was left of it would surely be eaten by the ocean's natural scavengers or sink into the depths to rot. The two remaining ships of the task force were a good hour out from the scene of the battle already, and Robbins wasn't going back.

Robbins wanted to send Hydely over to the *Rom* so that the doctor could be Blanton's headache. Lieutenant Nicholson was a part of Blanton's direct command and should have been over there anyway. Robbins liked Nicholson. The lieutenant was professional and very competent. Those were traits Robbins valued in any officer.

Since he wasn't able to send Dr. Hydely over to the *Rom*, Nicholson was all that kept Robbins from tossing the doctor into the ocean, if truth be told. Hydely was the worst, most self-centered jerk Robbins had ever met. He had no idea how Nicholson hadn't shot the bastard already himself. It was again a testament to just how professional of an officer Nicholson was.

Upon denying Hydely's requests for what seemed like the thousandth time, Robbins ordered Nicholson to take the doctor to the megalodon control lab and keep him there. It kept Hydely out of his way other than the annoying comms calls, and Nicholson assured that it somewhat kept the doctor distracted too. Down there, Hydely could at least pretend like he was still working and doing something important so that the man's giant ego was satiated.

"Sir," the on-duty sonar tech said, motioning to him. Robbins could see from the expression David wore that something was up. He walked over to the sonar station to see what David wanted.

"I'm picking up some strange contacts, sir," David told him.

"Let me take a look, son," Robbins ordered. David got out of his seat to clear the way for Robbins as the former XO sat down at the sonar station. The glitches with the sonar had cleared up with the death of the Kraken. The system was working perfectly again. Robbins studied the hundreds of tiny dots on the screen wondering what in the devil they were. He ran a fast diagnostic just to be sure that the sonar was working as well as he had been told it was. The system checked out. Robbins leaned closer to the sonar screen trying to make sense of what he was seeing. His sonar tech was wrong. The number of contacts wasn't in the hundreds, it was in the thousands. He had seen something like these signatures before and he knew it. Then it hit him. Robbins leaped to his feet, leaving the sonar station's chair spinning behind him.

"All hands, action stations!" he yelled at his bridge crew. "And someone get me Commodore Blanton on the line. Now!"

****

The squids came by the hundreds. They swam just under the surface of the waves at a speed close to thirty knots. The bulk of them were eight feet long in length, though there were larger ones among their ranks. The largest of them ran fifteen feet or more in length from one end to the other. The Kraken had apparently given birth to them before its last engagement with the task force.

Blanton knew the squids wanted blood, his blood and that of the crews of the *Rom* and the *Leary*. Whether they were driven by a need for vengeance or hunger didn't matter. They were coming, and there would be Hell to pay when they reached the task force.

Both the *Rom* and the *Leary* were low on ammo for their weapon systems. The battles with the Kraken had drained their available resources greatly without even considering the amount of munitions that each ship had donated to be loaded aboard the *Harrell*. The squids were approaching from the south, which put them to the rear of the two ships. Both of the *Rom*'s aft torpedo launchers were offline for repairs, and the bulk of her deck missile launchers sat empty. Blanton knew that the C.I.W.S. alone likely wouldn't be enough to stop the squids. No, this battle was going to be decided on the very decks of his ship.

"Have Major Kessler get his men ready," Blanton told Glenn, his new acting XO.

Glenn nodded.

"And tell Kessler to break everything we've got out of the armory. I want every person on this ship who can hold and use a gun to have one. This could get ugly very quickly if Kessler and his men aren't able to keep those things from getting in here with us."

Blanton was thankful for all the nonessential entry points to the *Rom*'s interior had been closed off and welded shut the day before. Not even monsters like those squids could tear through the metal doors and bulkheads of the ship, or at least he prayed they couldn't.

Using the ship's exterior security cameras, Blanton watched Kessler and his men deploy along the length of the *Rom*. The number of men Kessler had was limited, so Glenn had volunteered to accompany them along with a group of non-essential personnel. Kessler hadn't been happy about it. He had mumbled something about babysitting before Blanton had made it clear that Glenn and the others were going with him regardless. Kessler had assigned Glenn and the volunteers in groups of two to each of the less-secured doorways leading into the interior of the ship.

The *Rom* hadn't been able to engage the squids at a distance, but the *Leary* sure had. She had gotten off several volleys of torpedoes before the squids got close to the point of making such weapons too dangerous to be used. The squids were small, fast targets, however. Blanton estimated that the torpedoes had taken out around twenty-five percent of the squids on their approach. It was enough to thin their numbers, but not enough to stop them.

The squids reached the *Leary* a good three minutes before they reached the *Rom*. The *Leary*'s C.I.W.S. had hammered the monsters with a virtual wall of high-velocity rounds, reducing their numbers even further, but it hadn't been able to stop them from boarding the ship.

Blanton had watched as the squids swarmed the *Leary*. They raced up the sides of the hull at impossible speeds and launched themselves onto her decks. It was like watching ants in summer time as they went after a piece of roadkill. Their numbers appeared endless. In less than a minute, all Blanton could see of the *Leary*'s side and deck from his viewpoint were the bodies of the squids.

The *Rom* had lost contact with the *Leary* only a minute later. There was nothing Blanton could do to help Robbins and his crew. The squids were already at his proverbial doorstep, too.

****

The thunder of the *Rom*'s C.I.W.S. fell quiet. It had fired its final rounds and now slumped, useless in its turret. It had done a great deal of damage to the approaching squids. The waters surrounding the ship were black with the oil-like blood of the squids. Kessler could still see far too many squids moving in the water on their way to the *Rom* to even attempt to venture a guess at their numbers.

Kessler cursed as the squids reached the *Rom* and began to climb the sides of the hull. They came like some sort of demented ice-climbers. They would fling one of their primary tentacles out and upwards, its hook burying itself in the metal of the side of the ship, use it to pull themselves up, and then repeat the process. They moved with blinding speed. Even as Kessler's men opened fire, machine guns, shotguns, and pistols blazing, the first squids were already coming over the deck railing.

Jerking up the barrel of his M-16, Kessler let the closest squid to him have a three-round blast at near point-blank range. The bullets rip and tore their way through its central body, spraying black blood in the air. The squid toppled to the deck, its body twitching about in death throes.

Kessler was a veteran and knew the battle had already been lost. The squids were just too many. He wanted to order his men to fall back, but there was nowhere to fall back to. He and his men were cut off and flanked by the squids. If Kessler wanted to get inside the *Rom*, he and his men would have to fight a path through the squids surrounding them to do so. So instead, Kessler made the call for his men to stand their ground. The battle was a short and bloody one.

In the distance, Kessler could hear the grenades of other groups of his soldiers detonating among the ranks of the squids. Trapped as his men were on the *Rom*'s port side, the quarters were too close for such tactics here. He watched one of his men take down a squid with a pump-action shotgun. The squid's central mass all but disintegrated as the heavy blast slammed into it. Another of his men was carrying a mini-gun. Its barrels spun, hosing the squids coming up from the bow of the ship with a continuous stream of fire that tore them to shreds by the dozens.

The soldier with the mini-gun screamed as a squid dropped onto him. Its weight and the man's panicked response took them both to the deck. The squid sat atop the soldier, slashing him repeatedly with the tips of its primary tentacles and continued to do so long after the man was dead.

The squids hadn't just climbed the sides of the ship that led up from the water. They were all over her now. Kessler's mouth hung open as he looked up at where the squid had just dropped from to see dozens more scurrying in a sideways motion on the walls above the position of his men. He didn't even have time to scream as one the monsters threw itself from the wall down onto him. One of its tentacles whipped out to hit him directly in his open mouth, its tip emerging from the base of his neck in an explosion of red.

****

Blanton saw that Kessler and his men had lost the exterior decks of the *Rom* via the ship's security cameras. There were reports coming in from all over that the squids were inside the *Rom*'s internal corridors. Blanton had the entrance to the bridge sealed but knew it wouldn't hold. If the things had been able to tear the inside the ship, one more door wasn't going to stop them. At most, it would buy him and his bridge crew a few more minutes of life.

Blanton looked around the bridge. Only his helmsman, Greg, and two other officers remained on it. Everyone else had been sent to help stop the squids. Greg and the others were armed. An M-16 rested propped against the helm next to where Greg sat. Blanton, himself, wore a pistol holstered on his hip. He drew it as he heard something bang against the bridge's sealed entrance.

Hydely had been right about how fast the Kraken could create new spawn it seemed. Though they had destroyed the Mother

Kraken, Blanton was forced to wonder if these lesser squids could reproduce as well. If so, the Earth's oceans would never be the same. They would be the power on the waves and the masters of the depths. And given how quickly they reproduced and their ability to move about out of the water, the human race might just be facing its final war.

Blanton thought about his home. He envisioned his yard filled with squids loping about on their two primary tentacles as if they were legs. In his mind's eye, he saw his house burning as the squids danced about wildly in front of it. That vision expanded as he beheld Washington, D.C. overrun, people fleeing for their very lives in its streets, the sides of the city's buildings swarming with squids. Broken and battered tanks sat motionless in among overturned and abandoned cars.

Shaking his head to chase away the nightmares of his thoughts, Blanton heard the thrashing outside the door to the bridge growing louder. Blanton imagined the squids on the other side of the door, their numbers being added to more and more of the creatures following those already there in search of still-living prey. Some of the blows against the door dented it, bending its metal inward to protrude out towards the bridge's interior.

"Sir!" Blanton heard Greg yell and turned to see what had so frightened the helmsman.

The bridge's forward window was a mass of squids. They blocked the view of the ocean completely. All that could be seen were tentacles writhing and twisting about against the glass, pushing into it in an attempt to break through it.

"God have mercy on our souls," Blanton muttered as the window shattered and the squids came bursting through it.

FIN

Eric S Brown is the author of numerous book series including the Bigfoot War series, the Kaiju Apocalypse series (with Jason Cordova), the Crypto-Squad series (with Jason Brannon), the Homeworld series (With Tony Faville and Jason Cordova), the Jack Bunny Bam series, and the A Pack of Wolves series. Some of his stand alone books include War of the Worlds plus Blood Guts and Zombies, World War of the Dead, Last Stand in a Dead Land, Sasquatch Lake, Kaiju Armageddon, Megalodon, Megalodons, and Megalodon Apocalypse to name only a few. His short fiction has been published hundreds of times in the small press in beyond including markets like the Onward Drake and Black Tide Rising anthologies from Baen Books, the Grantville Gazette, the SNAFU Military horror anthology series, and Walmart World magazine. He has done the novelizations for such films as Boggy Creek: The Legend is True (Studio 3 Entertainment) and The Bloody Rage of Bigfoot (Great Lake films). The first book of his Bigfoot War series was adapted into a feature by Origin Releasing in 2014. Werewolf Massacre at Hell's Gate was the second his books to be adapted into film in 2015. In addition to his fiction, Eric also writes an award winning comic book news column entitled "Comics in a Flash." Eric lives in North Carolina with his wife and two children where he continues to write tales of the hungry dead, blazing guns, and the things that lurk in the woods.

CHECK OUT OTHER GREAT
DEEP SEA THRILLERS

THEY RISE
by Hunter Shea

Some call them ghost sharks, the oldest and strangest looking creatures in the sea.

Marine biologist Brad Whitley has studied chimaera fish all his life. He thought he knew everything about them. He was wrong. Warming ocean temperatures free legions of prehistoric chimaera fish from their methane ice suspended animation. Now, in a corner of the Bermuda Triangle, the ocean waters run red. The 400 million year old massive killing machines know no mercy, destroying everything in their path. It will take Whitley, his climatologist ex-wife and the entire US Navy to stop them in the bloodiest battle ever seen on the high seas.

SERPENTINE
by Barry Napier

Clarkton Lake is a picturesque vacation spot located in rural Virginia, great for fishing, skiing, and wasting summer days away.

But this summer, something is different. When butchered bodies are discovered in the water and along the muddy banks of Clarkton Lake, what starts out as a typical summer on the lake quickly turns into a nightmare.

This summer, something new lives in the lake...something that was born in the darkest depths of the ocean and accidentally brought to these typically peaceful waters.

It's getting bigger, it's getting smarter...and it's always hungry.

CHECK OUT OTHER GREAT DEEP SEA THRILLERS

SEA RAPTOR
by John J. Rust

From terrorist hunter to monster hunter! Jack Rastun was a decorated U.S. Army Ranger, until an unfortunate incident forced him out of the service. He is soon hired by the Foundation for Undocumented Biological Investigation and given a new mission, to search for cryptids, creatures whose existence has not been proven by mainstream science. Teaming up with the daring and beautiful wildlife photographer Karen Thatcher, they must stop a sea monster's deadly rampage along the Jersey Shore. But that's not the only danger Rastun faces. A group of murderous animal smugglers also want the creature. Rastun must utilize every skill learned from years of fighting, otherwise, his first mission for the FUBI might very well be his last.

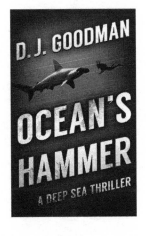

OCEAN'S HAMMER
by D.J. Goodman

Something strange is happening in the Sea of Cortez. Whales are beaching for no apparent reason and the local hammerhead shark population, previously believed to be fished to extinction, has suddenly reappeared. Marine biologists Maria Quintero and Kevin Hoyt have come to investigate with a television producer in tow, hoping to get footage that will land them a reality TV show. The plan is to have a stand-off against a notorious illegal shark-fishing captain and then go home.

Things are not going according to plan.

There is something new in the waters of the Sea of Cortez. Something smart. Something huge. Something that has its own plans for Quintero and Hoyt.

CHECK OUT OTHER GREAT DEEP SEA THRILLERS

MEGATOOTH
by Viktor Zarkov

When the death rate of sperm whales rises dramatically, a well-respected environmental activist puts together a ragtag team to hit the high seas to investigate the matter. They suspect that the deaths are due to poachers and they are all driven by a need for justice.

Elsewhere, an experimental government vessel is enhancing deep sea mining equipment. They see one of these dead whales up close and personal...and are fairly certain that it wasn't poachers that killed it.

Both of these teams are about to discover that poachers are the least of their worries. There is something hunting the whales...

Something big
Something prehistoric.
Something terrifying.
MEGATOOTH!

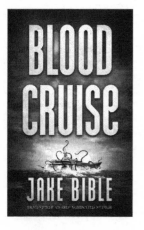

BLOOD CRUISE
by Jake Bible

Ben Clow's plans are set. Drop off kids, pick up girlfriend, head to the marina, and hop on best friend's cruiser for a weekend of fun at sea. But Ben's happy plans are about to be changed by a tentacled horror that lurks beneath the waves.

International crime lords! Deep cover black ops agents! A ravenous, bloodsucking monster! A storm of evil and danger conspire to turn Ben Clow's vacation from a fun ocean getaway into a nightmare of a Blood Cruise!

CHECK OUT OTHER GREAT
DEEP SEA THRILLERS

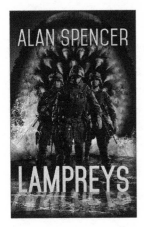

LAMPREYS
by Alan Spencer

A secret government tactical team is sent to perform a clean sweep of a private research installation. Horrible atrocities lurk within the abandoned corridors. Mutated sea creatures with insane killing abilities are waiting to suck the blood and meat from their prey.

Unemployed college professor Conrad Garfield is forced to assist and is soon separated from the team. Alone and afraid, Conrad must use his wits to battle mutated lampreys, infected scientists and go head-to-head with the biggest monstrosity of all.

Can Conrad survive, or will the deadly monsters suck the very life from his body?

DEEP DEVOTION
by M.C. Norris

Rising from the depths, a mind-bending monster unleashes a wave of terror across the American heartland. Kate Browning, a Kansas City EMT confronts her paralyzing fear of water when she traces the source of a deadly parasitic affliction to the Gulf of Mexico. Cooperating with a marine biologist, she travels to Florida in an effort to save the life of one very special patient, but the source of the epidemic happens to be the nest of a terrifying monster, one that last rose from the depths to annihilate the lost continent of Atlantis.

Leviathan, destroyer, devoted lifemate and parent, the abomination is not going to take the extermination of its brood well.

CHECK OUT OTHER GREAT
DEEP SEA THRILLERS

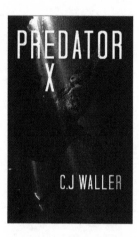

PREDATOR X
by C.J Waller

When deep level oil fracking uncovers a vast subterranean sea, a crack team of cavers and scientists are sent down to investigate. Upon their arrival, they disappear without a trace. A second team, including sedimentologist Dr Megan Stoker, are ordered to seek out Alpha Team and report back their findings. But Alpha team are nowhere to be found – instead, they are faced with something unexpected in the depths. Something ancient. Something huge. Something dangerous. Predator X

DEAD BAIT
by Tim Curran

A husband hell-bent on revenge hunts a Wereshark...A Russian mail order bride with a fishy secret...Crabs with a collective consciousness...A vampire who transforms into a Candiru...Zombie piranha...Bait that will have you crawling out of your skin and more. Drawing on horror, humor with a helping of dark fantasy and a touch of deviance, these 19 contemporary stories pay homage to the monsters that lurk in the murky waters of our imaginations. If you thought it was safe to go back in the water...Think Again!

 SEVEREDPRESS

CHECK OUT OTHER GREAT DEEP SEA THRILLERS

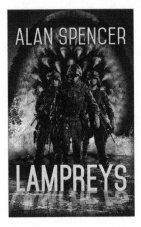

LAMPREYS
by Alan Spencer

A secret government tactical team is sent to perform a clean sweep of a private research installation. Horrible atrocities lurk within the abandoned corridors. Mutated sea creatures with insane killing abilities are waiting to suck the blood and meat from their prey.
Unemployed college professor Conrad Garfield is forced to assist and is soon separated from the team. Alone and afraid, Conrad must use his wits to battle mutated lampreys, infected scientists and go head-to-head with the biggest monstrosity of all.
Can Conrad survive, or will the deadly monsters suck the very life from his body?

DEEP DEVOTION
by M.C. Norris

Rising from the depths, a mind-bending monster unleashes a wave of terror across the American heartland. Kate Browning, a Kansas City EMT confronts her paralyzing fear of water when she traces the source of a deadly parasitic affliction to the Gulf of Mexico. Cooperating with a marine biologist, she travels to Florida in an effort to save the life of one very special patient, but the source of the epidemic happens to be the nest of a terrifying monster, one that last rose from the depths to annihilate the lost continent of Atlantis.

Leviathan, destroyer, devoted lifemate and parent, the abomination is not going to take the extermination of its brood well.

35376645R00080

Made in the USA
Middletown, DE
30 September 2016